TONY DI NAPOLI

Frank Palescandolo
Sorrento
2000

TONY DI NAPOLI

A Novel of the Lower East Side

Frank Palescandolo

iUniverse, Inc.
New York Lincoln Shanghai

Tony Di Napoli
A Novel of the Lower East Side

iUniverse, Inc.

For information address:
iUniverse, Inc.
2021 Pine Lake Road, Suite 100
Lincoln, NE 68512
www.iuniverse.com

Author photo by courtesy of Antonino De Angelis

ISBN: 0-595-27105-7

Printed in the United States of America

For

East Siders

and

their progeny

CHAPTER 1

1930

Damp snows of March fell and watered away on the steaming haunches of the double team of horses Tony was driving for Patsy Paglieri, the undertaker on First Avenue. His father's ice wagon horse Jim was in the shafts on loan for funerals. He was not sheer black. Tony rubbed black shoe polish on a white blaze on his head which showed when the bridle rubbed against it. After three hours drive from the East Side, the cortege halted a mile away from Calvary Cemetery in Queens in front of Loughran's saloon, the fourth saloon stop since the Mass at St. Anne's Cathedral that morning. It was a custom, the day was dismally gray, mourners and coachmen deserved a vitalizer. Patsy's livery teams recognized the saloon stops along the route, and now halted, the last of the journey. While the mourners and coachmen thronged the bar with clouded breaths, Patsy gave the horses a snortfull of whiskey that stung frozen muzzles. A mean March, the flu was raging in the city causing a shortage of coffins, or enough coaches, drivers, and horses to serve the traffic of the epidemic dead. Patsy hired Tony's father's old dray Jim, and eighteen year Tony himself, who was driving the young widow's coach. The corpse lies in plain box for lack of a coffin. He rose one morning to got to work at Mori's restaurant in Greenwich Village. He was in line for the better tables and well liked, too, by the patrons.

When he arrived home to his bride of three months, he was found dead on the granite stoop. Everyone but the young widow piled into the saloon, she remained apart with her private sorrow in the leading coach after the hearse. No amount of urging could convince her to join the mourners at the bar, to curse the chill, and the fate that brought her here to Calvary Cemetery. She was wearing her wedding dress of white organdy bought on Delancey Street, a veil, and a three month old faded corsage of yellowed gardenias. She fought mother, aunts, father, her priest, she would not wear black, she would throw herself into the open grave to embrace her young spouse on a darker honeymoon. All the mourners sighed, they thought of her, alone in the coach, freezing in her frilly bridal gown. Tears glistening, solid pearls on her cheeks. O dear! And, they ordered another round.

Tony tethered the horses, stood watch over the coaches while Patsy joined the others at the bar. Passing the coach of the widow he heard whimpers, and shivering cries. He opened the door, the bridal widow was huddled in a corner of the patchy velvet lined coach. She stared back, defiantly.

"Go, go, go away!" she managed to say. Tony swore her tongue was frozen, too.

Tony closed the door, on the run he crashed the party at the bar, all gloom lifted, the jabbering had turned to merrier wakes. He asked the bartender for any drink to warm the widow. A tumbler of cherry brandy was slid to him along the bartop. At this point, the dispensing was done now in heavy tumblers, no temperate shot glasses. He rushed back to the widow's coach, opened it boldly, stepped in. If he did not revive her, Tony was sure she would follow her dead spouse into the grave, she was turning blue. The organdy had stiffened in the freezing and spiked about her body. He said not a word, mercifully mum, afraid he would emit a cry out of pity. He knew the bride, a pert redhead, his sister said she was one of the good girls of the neighborhood. He extended the tumbler of cherry brandy. She glared at him suspiciously. The cherry brandy appeared to smoke its warmth and fragrance in the confined coach. She reached for it with cramped fingers, and gulped a mouthful.

"I hope it kills me!"

"It ain't poison."

"I wish it was!"

"Sip it slow, slow."

"Only drinking it so I am alive to throw myself into the grave."

Tony looked away.

"Look at me. I saw a tear in your eyes."

"The cold snap waters eyes."

She sipped again. Color began to return to her cheeks. "You feel sorry for me, that's the reason."

Tony wiped his eyes with a forearm. "You are so young."

"And you, too." She remembered him when he delivered ice and coal to the cold water flats in hot summers to help out his father. She never paid real attention, she was in love with Arturo.

Since she first saw Tony hauling chunks of ice, he was taller, more manful, his black curly hair was frosted white, wide shoulders were free of the burlap where the pennnie's worth of ice rested.

"You are used to the cold," she said.

"I always hated ice. My name is Tony."

"Thank you, Tony, so I can stand at the edge of his grave, and jump."

"I did not bring you the brandy to let that happen. You must live."

She emptied the last of the brandy. "So you too think I am crazy to wear this dress at his funeral?" She uncrossed her long legs, and sidled nearer along the cushion of the coach.

"Man and wife barely three months! No time to put the dress away in a box with mothballs, to save for anniversaries. You remember Arturo, how handsome he was, so proud waiting at Mori's, that red cummerbund across his waist, how he flicked his napkin across his arm. I can see him now—and now—he will be buried in a nailed box, no coffins, without a pillow. In a bare box he is colder than all of us." She had a fit of shivering, she held out her arms to hold her, to stop the shivering. Tony moved closer, opened his mackinaw to provide the warmth of his sweater and held her close.

"O! If only I can hold him as you hold me now, to press him with the warmth of my breast, my breath, to kiss him as I kiss you now." She began to kiss him blindly. He pulled away.

"No! Don't leave me again Arturo caro! Stay close, closer, like our wedding night, Arturo! Arturo! Kiss me as when you made my toes curl with passion."

Tony drew back.

"No! No! Arturo! Don't leave me again, don't die, Arturo, you are alive. Make love to me."

She leaned against Tony, forcing him to lie back on the seat. She was astride him, biting his lips, kissing his cheeks, his eyes, his brow, his chin, his throat, kissing the pulsing arteries of his neck. He tried to rise her body fully upon him, her pelvis against his groin. She fumbled with his pants while calling his name Arturo! Arturo! My God! he was penetrating her!

"O Arturo! O Arturo!" She moaned and fell back languorously. Her eyelids were fluttering like twin butterflies dying. Tony rubbed her naked limbs to revive her. He slipped his hand through a corselet to feel her heart, under hard nipples and rounded breasts it beat erratically.

She opened her eyes, dazed, she asked, "Who are you?"

Tony heard Patsy's voice calling him, the bar stop was over, the cortege was ready to go on to Calvary. He shed his mackinaw and laid it across her body. When he clambered down from the coach, Patsy looked at him puzzled, looked into the coach, he then flicked his whip across Tony's ass.

"*Mascalzone*! Bad boy!" he said with a wink and a chuckle.

CHAPTER 2

Back to the East Side, now raining in sleety gusts. The young widow got off at a tenement on East Eleventh Street. She finally balked at the edge of the grave. The empty coaches headed for Patsy Paglieri's livery stable on East Twelfth Street next to Montone's blacksmith shop. Missing the mackinaw on the body of the widow, and divested of the mourning cloak supplied by the undertaker, Tony wore heavy twilled pants, a woolen shirt, a frayed sweater, and his father's suspenders. He welcomed the animal warmth of the stable. He debated if he should visit the widow to reclaim the mackinaw, the only one he owned. Patsy was at his shoulder.

"Tony, I know what happened back there. You keep away from her! I know you are a good boy, she say you took advantage of her, and she has brothers. *Capisce?*"

"My mackinaw."

"Tony, the coach has springs, up and down, I hear her pleasure. You listen good, she is *pazzo.*"

Patsy grabbed a cap from a peg that belonged to an ostler and placed it on Tony's head. He stood back to take a long look at Tony. *Oggi,* today, he was a man, he heard a deeper voice, saw a strong jaw, broad shoulders, taller than an Irish cop, a high brow that ended in a widow's peak, curly black hair, a gap-toothed smile that gave a whimsical charm to his rugged features, his eyes were large and sorrowful. *Bello!*

"You catch cold warming women, your father say what you do to my son, eh?" He handed Tony eight quarters, his pay for the day. Tony placed the soiled cap that teetered on his springy hair, and thanked the undertaker. He unhooked the shafts from the worn out Jim, and began to lead him back to his stable near the East River on First Avenue. He borrowed a canvas cover to shield Jim still steaming from the long haul to Calvary Cemetery. Afternoon on First Avenue, both sides of the streets were lined with pushcarts selling vegetables, dry goods, toys, jewelry, second hand clothes, tended by women in bulky layers of rags, and quilts, heads covered with decorative shawls. Store windows were grimy, a succession of motley signs smeared the grey stone fronts. Unkempt children played hooky under pushcarts while a truant officer patrolled. He weaved Jim in and out of sidestreets, and corners hilled by dirty snow. The curb gutters were running off the early Spring melt. Jim sighted his stable and was off on a trot to his stall. There, Tony wiped him dry, filled his manger with hay, gave him a long drink at the trough, and pitchforked a bed of straw. He slapped Jim on the rump, and closed the stable door. On the way home he thought to treat himself to a hot espresso. Passing Veniero's pasticceria on Eleventh Street off First, he stepped in and ordered an espresso, and a pasticiotto. A two cent tip entitled him to a spurt of anisette in his brimming espresso. Under a gleaming showcase were tucked arrays of *babas, sfogliatelle, zeppoles, cassata, cannoli*, each in a doily, a bottom shelf held assorted cookies and biscotti. He bought his father's favorite *biscotti*, anise. The walls were mirrored reflecting the patrons sitting on wired chairs at marbled topped tables, on the counter wall were photos of prizes won by tiered wedding cakes at expositions, on which stood tiny effigies of groom and bride. To Tony, it looked like he, too, was a subject of a conditter's art of almond paste. The hissing of the foaming espresso machines and clink of china cups and saucers was music. A cozy place for dreaming in a marzipan palace perfumed by orange water, citron, vanilla, and clouds of powdered confectioner's sugar. On a nearby counter, a *gelatiere* was apportioning spumoni, in doing so he exposed the center compacted with fresh fruit and nougat cream.

While munching the pastry, he began to go over what happened that morning on the way to the cemetery. He must not forget to change his pants, wash away the semen stains in the communal zinc sink out of sight of his sister who did the wash for all. How could he explain if she suspected? Did his sister know of such things? It all happened so fast, it took longer when he masturbated! This time—whee! Teresa, who was only older by three years, or his father, would they notice any change? On the fifth landing of the Old-Law tenement, he heard his sister and father arguing in the dining room. He dashed by them, into the bedroom he shared with his father, stripped himself of his pants, placed it under the bed, and slipped on his Sunday trousers. Later, he could soak the work pants in the sink. He heard his name mentioned more than once. Had the widow complained to his father? Was he in trouble? How could he face his sister? He also heard the word City College. Did the widow complain to his Dean? He peeked. Teresa stood tall against the low ledged windows on a level with L tracks. Her dark hair springy like Tony's was disciplined into a large bun, her expression was always pensive, sweetly meditative. Her eyes were lustrous, Tony sometimes suspected a film of fever. The face a perfect oval as in old-fashioned cameos. When he entered the dining room his sister met him and hugged him tightly.

"Tony, don't listen to your father. No!" His father was sitting at the dining room table clinching a frayed Toscano cigar. He looked at Tony wearily.

"Papa, I got you some *biscotti.*"

"Sit down Tony, *figlio mio*, we must talk." Tony kissed his father and sat beside him. "Last week, you remember Tony, you give me a box of cigars on my birthday. I was fifty-five years old. Not an old age, sure, but look at me *figlio mio bello*, my back is hunched, my breath is short, my legs, they shake when I pick up a bag of coal. This morning I bring a fifty cents bag of coal to Mrs. Golub, number forty nine, when I fell on my knees before the stove. Mrs. Golub help me to stand up."

"What is wrong, Dominick?" she say.

"I no answer Tony, no breath in my chest. She bring chair, I sit down catch my breath, my heart she go thump-thump. She give me a sweet wine to drink. I drink. I feel better, not better to put the coal away. She pick up bag of coal and put in scuttle. I watch, I say to myself, Dominick, when a woman does my work, then I no working man."

Tony's sister hid her tears behind some drapery of the window that looked out on the L tracks of the Second Avenue subway.

"All today, I do street floor, I no climb stairs, I miss 36, 83, 90, 55, 32, and I forget—so you see, my son, I have no business."

"Hell with the business, Papa, it's you we must think of!"

"Tony, you care your sister. I an old sick man, and cannot put bread no more on the table, or save for her dowry."

In the past months Tony was so taken up with exams at City College in his sophomore year, he neglected his father. A silent sob twisted his chest, he saw his father as he was, thinner, his jowls were sunken, his back bowed, his mustache drooped whitened by a line of froth from his lips, he held one hand tightly to keep it from trembling. Tony fell at his knees and embraced him tightly. "Every summer you on vacation, you work with me, Tony. Everybody like you, you are strong like me when I your age."

His sister spoke, "Tony—he is trying to tell you you must quit school and take over the business to support me. He says does not matter anymore, he will die soon." She wrung her hands. "You are the only Italian boy in the neighborhood who is going to City College!"

Dominick prodded Tony to rise, and sit again beside him. "You know I send you to school, I no say you go to work, no—but now who pay the rent? I got 245 dollars in the Dime Savings Bank, your sister, she keep account good. Pretty soon old Jim die like me, you need new horse. I thank you for the honor of going to school, what I ask is only short time, you take over business, you make money, bury me honorably and take care of your sister until she get married, then you sell business, go back to school. I bite my tongue with every word I say. Blood in my mouth."

"Sure, Papa, I leave school until you get better, then I go back to school. It is all settled."

"You see, Teresa, she get married."

"You both know I can't get married even if someone wanted me, I have questionable spots on my lungs, Doctor Nash warned me. I had to leave Nanina's dress shop because of the lint, bad for my lungs, but I can get a job, Tony can stay in school on the Dean's list! We can manage."

Dominick shook his head. "Who give money for new Jim, wagon need wheel—"

"Listen Sis, Papa is right, it is killing him to say what he is saying, tomorrow I go to school, sign myself out and see if my credits can be advanced to next semester."

"I swear on all the angels in heaven and St. Anne, you will finish school. I will get a job tomorrow." She began to cough and ran to open a window on a rumbling train.

"Sis, you stay home, and no job until Doctor Nash gives you the go ahead. You take care of Papa, I take over the route. I'll stop by school to sign out."

Dominick banged the table with his fist. "I fail you both!"

CHAPTER 3

All settled, he was a man, in repeat with each roaring rumble of the L train by his window. He was awake nightlong. When the day dawned with the first rays, he was anointed, the head of the household, protector of his sister, Tessie, supporter of his ailing father, and he had had a woman. What was his advent day, he glanced at the kitchen calendar above the wood kindling for the coal stove. March 11,1930. The clock nearby read four a.m., time to get going, to hitch Jim to the ice wagon for the trip to the Hudson River where he would soon hear the whirr of the saws cutting blocks of the frozen river to load on his wagon. Half a wagon would be enough, a clear bitter day from the looks of the frosted windows of the bedroom he shared with his father. Dominick voyaged America in 1900 alone, his first job was seasonal ice harvesting on the Hudson above Nyack. A grid was marked on the frozen river after snow was scraped off by horse-drawn teams. A hole was cut in the ice to allow hand cutting saws to segment the ice into floatable cakes that were moved on by prods along a channel to the waiting horse-drawn sleighs to be delivered to a nearby depot. One season, an icehouse burned down which was hard to imagine, cakes of ice were separated by layers of straw hay, or sawdust, to avoid an iceberg in the ice house. His father said Nyack had a cool summer. He listened to his father's irregular breathing, a catch at each breath.

He will bring his father to see Doctor Nash at the clinic at the Bellevue Hospital. From habit, Dominick, roused himself, he was sitting up, groping in the dark for his pants.

"Papa, stay in bed, rest, it's my turn." He eased his father back into a prone position, and raised the covers to his chin.

"What people say they don't see Dominick?"

"I tell them Dominick downtown to get citizenship papers, everybody say hurray for Dominick."

"I dream of Mama, she die in this bed."

Tony passed a hand over his eyes to block that sight of his mother dying of uterine cancer in the same bed three years ago.

"What happen summer when district leader have picnic Ulmer, no Dominick to cool the beer kegs with shaved ice."

"You'll be there, Papa."

"Go easy with old Jim. In my pants sugar, here you give to old Jim from Dominick."

"How many bags of coal must I pick up at the yard?"

"Three, *figlio mio bello*, and four blocks of ice."

"I'll wake up Tessie before I leave."

"No, first start fire in coal stove so she be warm when she gets up, or she start coughing."

"Rest, Papa, rest." He laid his hand on father's forehead, drew back in alarm, the skin was marble cold. He fired up the kitchen stove with the kindling from fruit crates, and did not leave until the plate was red hot. He placed a kettle of water on the hot plate for Tessie's tea, and Papa's black coffee. He laid the fresh biscotti by his father's cup.

Two hours later Tony was on the ice dock loading from an enormous ice house whose walls were thick as a fortress, filled with insulating cork. An ice house burned down a year ago, all fireworks as the walls crumbled releasing granulated cork chips which caught fire to become flaming scintillae that lit up the city sky. He and Teresa watched from the roof. His father was not spoofing when he said an ice house can catch fire and melt.

A stop at the coal yard, and he was loaded, a tug at the right rein and Jim's hooves pointed in well trotted direction to the East Side tenements that bordered Fourteenth Street and Canal. Soon Jim was trotting along Second Avenue, and stopped on cue in front of the Café Royale. You lugged the ice through the Vienna coffee house entrance to get to the kitchen first, then the bar. The cafe did not open until eight, so the chairs were arranged seat down on the round tables, and waiters were sweeping the floor.

Emil Sommers was the proprietor, a stout, kindly man who spoke with an accent. Tony delivered ice here during summer heat waves, even then, the delivery was only two cakes of ice. The patrons drink wine, or hard liquor, Tokay, Reislings, Slivovitz, and Pilsners in bottles, or ale at cellar temperature. That summer he delivered an emergency load of three cakes in a heat wave when the cafe was busiest at noontime. He understood later the cafe was a Bohemian hangout for artists, refugees, intellectuals of every stripe, and anarchists, you could tell the anarchists, they wore flamboyant, telltale red bow ties, or red cravats. What confused Tony was the high volume of talk in languages of many nationalities at the outdoor tables, all speaking a fanfaronade of language, Hungarian, German, Russian, Italian, Yiddish. As he passed by, someone stuck a book in his pocket, and poked him encouragingly, a book by the Italian anarchist Enrico Malatesta. He astonished his civic teacher in his junior year by tossing off the names of Engels, Bakunin, Neitzche, Kropotkin, and Heine. One reason why Tony, in addition, to a heavy program in advance math, chose German an elective, so he could read the originals. On these drops, patrons often spoke to him in an Italian he did not understand, he spoke a pidgin Neapolitan dialect in halting phrases. Italian was not taught at City College. On warm evenings, he and Teresa stopped by to listen to a concert of waltzes, polkas, and mazurkas. He had to restrain Teresa from dancing in the street.

Often, a forty pound chunk of ice on his shoulders, he was waylaid by a patron who harangued him, or asked him to choose sides, as the ice melted across his shoulders. When he got to the spacious kitchen, he climbed a ladder to the top opening of the walk-in icebox to unload the ice on a platform which allowed cooling for the perishables below.

This morning Emil Sommers, who was also a pastry chef, while fixing an apron across an ample waist asked, "Where's your father, Dominick?" He recognized Tony from last summer.

"Citizenship papers."

"Good man your father, you strong like him."

"I am helping."

"I see, I see, you good son too, here is a *schnecken* hot from the oven."

"Thank you, Mr. Sommers."

"When Dominick become citizen, we celebrate, eh? I will bake a torte with American flag, you think that nice?"

"Thank you, I'll tell him when I go home."

"You tell him president of United States Mr. Herbert Hoover, so he make no mistake."

Tony shared the cinnamon bun with Jim.

Tony had unfinished deliveries on the wagon, the coal would keep, but a cake of ice had to be sacrificed. He trotted Jim to City College to ask his Dean for a leave of absence. The school was in full session, his heart sank as the sharp reality of actually quitting school struck him. He tied Jim to a lamp post, and took the stairs slowly at the main entrance. On the first floor, he ran into his math advisor and coach of the math team Sol Horowitz. He glanced at Tony twice not recognizing him in his work clothes, Horowitz was a short wiry man of manic energy. Two students stood by with erasers to follow and erase his equations on the blackboard.

"Tony, I missed you in class this morning. Why the getup?"

"I must see the Dean, Mr. Horowitz."

"What for? Have you been sentenced to the galleys?"

"I got to quit school for a while, my father is sick, I must help out."

Now, Sol Horowitz was really disturbed. "What? You are about to graduate next semester! I won't stand for it!" he said with indignation. "We have a meet with Columbia next Saturday, and I am counting on you to trounce them. You can't do this to the team, no!" Then Sol Horowitz collected himself when he saw tears in Tony's eyes. "There must be a solution to your problem. Come I'll accompany you to the Dean's office. Perhaps we all can work out some alternative." He placed his arm over Tony's shoulder and Tony explained the crisis in the family as they walked to the Dean's office. Mr. Flynn, the Dean, looked up a bit perplexed, but smiling at Horowitz and his promising protégé, Anthony Di Napoli.

"Hello Tony, is that your wagon outside?"

"Yes, Mr. Flynn."

"You should be in class."

"Jim, Anthony has a problem, he must quit school."

"Preposterous, never heard of such a thing! I won't allow it! We have plans for him, as you well know."

"I have been talking to him, he is determined, or rather circumstances force him to this decision."

"I can't imagine anything more important than his remaining to graduate."

"His father is ill, cannot carry on the ice business, so Tony must sub for a while until he gets better. He requires a leave of absence."

The Dean rose from his chair to join Sol Horowitz and Tony, and suggested going to the teacher's cafeteria for coffee.

"Anthony, Sol Horowitz and I have done some planning for your academic future. We intended to tell you at graduation. We have considered you as valedictorian, more importantly, we have a fellowship opening for you on our math faculty."

Tony head drooped despairingly, and he stared at his shoes.

"You see Jim, his father is ill and sole support of the family and his sister is not well." He mouthed TB for the Dean's attention.

"Tony, I am sure this is a temporary situation, and things will right themselves. I'll authorize a leave for six months, we expect you back in the Fall. In the meantime I, and Mr. Horowitz will try to keep that fellowship alive. I hope your father recovers soon."

"Thank you both. Mr. Horowitz give my regrets to the team."

Tony found Jim balky and chewing at the halter to the lamp post, the school was an unfamiliar stop. As he was leaving, Tony saw the math team who had gathered on the school steps to wave to him.

That evening when he arrived at the flat Dominick was sitting up by the window. He had shaved and Teresa was trimming his hair, he appeared more relaxed and breathing easier. He was wearing a flow-ered robe given to him by Mr. Antonescu, the tailor on Second Ave near Houston Street, which had been left unclaimed after alterations. Dominick never had the leisure to wear it until now. Dominick rose to greet Tony, but Teresa set him down gently.

"Papa, sit still or I'll nip your ears."

"*Come andato, la giornata*, Antonio?"

"Had a good day, Papa. Everybody asking, "Where is Dominick? I told them you retired. They send you love and good luck."

"*Buona gente, buona gente* Antonio, my friends many years."

"Papa was good today, Tony. For lunch he had an omelet and a glass of wine. For dinner I'll make chicken soup with tagliatelle, and a piece of boiled chicken."

Dominick seemed to chew his words before he spoke haltingly.

"*Caro figlio bello*, you go to school?"

"Everything okay, Papa."

"You no sad?"

"Why sad, Papa, it's only temporary."

"Will you ever forgive me?"

Teresa threatened Dominick with her scissors, "If you don't stop this forgiving, I'll chop your ears off."

Dominick drew from the oversized pocket of the robe his blue book of accounts. "Antonio, you need my book, all my friends twenty years." He extended the book to Tony with a hint of ceremony and a trembling hand. "You take care of la *buona gente*."

"Remind me, Tony to review the entries I believe everyone is paid up to date."

"How is Jim, the sore heel on his leg?"

"He is fit as a fiddle."

"You give him sugar?"

"And a cinnamon bun."

"He like cinnamon."

"The day after tomorrow Dr. Nash will be a the clinic. Can you give us a lift in the morning, and pick us up later? I spoke to Dr. Nash on Laura's phone. He prescribed a mild stimulant which Mr. Santangelo, the pharmacist, delivered this morning late. It gave him a good appetite. Soon he'll be ready for his favorite rigatoni with ragu sauce and a braciole, eh Papa?"

"*Cara figlia, se dio vuole.*"

"I am doing the cooking, not God."

CHAPTER 4

Jim was between the shafts of the ice wagon, a polar light whitened the dawn, delivery this day was wood kindling, and coal. From under the seat he drew his father's thumb worn account book, soiled and stained. He began to read his rounds for the day, Tuesday 1930: The People's Theatre, The Russian Kretchma, Moe's candy store, Veniero's *pasticceria*, Birnbaum's bakery, Pulaski, Salerno, Abercrombie, De Fiore, Nussbaum, St. Mark's Church, Cleary, Sobieski, Dr. Henry Nash, Natale, van Brunts, Mollie's' millinery. A solo, his father Dominick, nowhere on the seat beside him handling the reins. Ambling only to the coal yard by the river, he had light, and the idling time to read deeper in his father's book. Fat like a worn out deck of playing cards. Here, Dominick listed his customers in barely literate hand. He read off Tuesday's stops, after each name was a series of three numbers—40, 17, 13 and 67, 89, 53,—which in Tony's recall had nothing to do with an address or money owed, and a scrawled notation of five cents, ten cents, twenty cents, rarely one dollar. In a separate column was the customary delivery of ice, coal, and kindling. And, many erasures that punctured pages. Tony saw two sets of books nor were they records of weekly payoffs to the racketeers who controlled the letting out of territories to the icemen of the city, which was five dollars monthly. Dominick's guaranteed territory was half of Lower Fourteenth Street, part of First Avenue, and

Gramercy Park. Plain to read except for the repetitive series of three numerals. Perhaps, Teresa knew the meaning of the entries, she kept the accounts, she never mentioned working off these entries. He gave her another account of the working day.

Fully loaded by ten in the morning he began his rounds, pulling out from the coal yard, Jim's hooves slipped on the slick Belgian cobblestones. Tony stepped down, grabbed the bridle to gain impetus until the wagon was rolling along the route. The De Fiore family was the first stop off Eleventh Street, three flights up an Old-Law tenement. Fifteen cents kindling, twenty cents worth of coal with a marginal note to dump in coal scuttle in hallway. Coal was delivered in a leather sack, capacious for all size orders. Often the anthracite nuggets fell out to tumble down a flight, or two. Always someone around to glean them.

He climbed the gray marble stairs scalloped by heavy use to the third floor. Loaded with the fardel of kindling, and coal, he tapped the bottom of the door with the toe guard of his father's work shoes. A small, cheery man opened the door and stepped aside to allow him to empty the coal into the scuttle. The man drew Tony into a lightless kitchen where Mr. De Fiore's face was sunny with good will. He began to prattle. "*Peccato*! I hear. I mean about your father, such a good man, when you come, my mother say you are good, too." Tony tapped his book. "Thank you, Mr. De Fiore. He spoke well of you also, of everyone."

"True, true, he had no enemies." Tony faced a long day, no time to chat with the engaging Mr. De Fiore. He waited for payment leaning towards the open door. Mr. De Fiore handed him 35 cents, and fifty cents separately calling out three numbers 34-66-43. Tony pocketed the coins and turned to leave.

"Domenico's son, write down the numbers, or you forget."

"Should I remember?"

"*Accidenti*! If you forget I lose the *terno*!"

Tony know understood what the numerical markings were all about, his father took lottery bets in the Italian lottery run by the Italian underworld! Never said a word to Tony! Was Teresa aware of his double bookkeeping?

"*Benedetto figlio di* Domenico, you know why your father he have no enemies?"

Tony heard a droning sound coming from an inner room. "My father spoke ill of no one."

De Fiore guffawed. "No, no—the reason I tell you so you have no enemies too."

"Thank you sir, for the nice things you say."

"Tony, you young, you do not understand life. No you wake up and say I make enemies today, no! Enemies are everywhere, in closets, on fire escapes, on the roof, in the street, in your shoes—they breathe the good air, and they breathe out malice and envy for no reason. Look at the saints, boiled, broiled, stabbed by enemies in the church itself! When you go home, enemies are on your doorstep crouching to do you harm. O! *la malvagita della gente*! Save us from the wicked!"

To calm the excitable man, Tony agreed. "I shall be careful, I was taught to listen to my elders."

"Domenico taught you well. Your father was protected from enemies, and you too on this day on. All are abominated before they do harm, you are being guarded against evil thoughts and deeds."

"Mr. De Fiore, you must pardon me, I have a new horse to break in and—"

He cocked an ear. "Listen good, Tony—"

That droning rose in volume and intensity. De Fiore placed a finger at his nose knowingly, "She knows you are here—"

"Who?"

"My mother, she is cursing your enemies. You say you have none? Listen!" The droning became more intense, sharper. He clapped his hands, "She has discovered them, not many, she is destroying them this very moment, cursing them to damnation!" The droning began to diminish. "Tony, you are free of enemies today! But whenever you come my mother will rid you of enemies. *Badate!* They spring up every day, poor woman, she has no rest. You have her dark blessing, I can tell. A word of warning, be wary of cracks in the sidewalk, under floorboards, or under your bed. Go, go forward, do your duty as a good son. Next time you come, you bring my mother a panforte from Veniero's to thank her."

"I shall Mr. De Fiore." At the door Mr. De Fiore said playfully, "About the *panforte*, she don't like chocolate."

He paused halfway down the stairs. He accepted the money for the lottery play. Should he go back to return it? He dreaded going back to listen to that infernal droning. Well, he could find someone to play off the number. He would ask Patsy about a lottery runner. That settled, he stopped the wagon at Mrs. Hyman's off East Eleventh Street. The standard order was a bag of coal, one dollars worth. Mrs. Hyman answered the door knock, a handsome stout woman in her mid-forties, large green eyes and tinted, Titian hair indifferently loose and bosomy waist. Her brassy voice was unnaturally loud, and her breath was cloyed with sweetness. She sized him up with vampish interest. "And-who are you, working your way through school?"

"I am Tony, Dominick's son."

"And, where is Dominick?"

"He is ill some days ago."

"Oi Vey! What a sorrow! Come in, come in, set down the coal by the stove. Stand by the window, let me look at you, you are a *mensch*!" She circled him. "Such shoulders, your hair like Valentino." She fingered his arms. "So strong!" She emitted a long sigh that sweetened the air. Tony saw the reason, a half empty bottle of Manichevitz wine on the table. Tony set back by the boldness of Mrs. Hyman, he stepped back into the hallway sensing a vague unpleasantness. She blocked him with her bosom, and raised her hands in protest.

"Such in a hurry! Have a glass of wine first, Tony, no sun, the flat is chilly, it warms you against the ice."

"No ice today, coal, Mrs. Hyman. No, thank you."

She poured a tumbler full. "But yes, Tony, you beautiful man-boy! Call me Minna."

She poured for herself, drank it down, then waited with an amusing eye for Tony to down his, which Tony did, impatient to get back on the route. She gave her shapely body a spin, to mimic a pirouette. "I buy my wine now. When I danced in the old cafes of Hungary, I never paid for a glass, young Hussars toasted me with slivovitz kummel and French champagne! You see how it is now, Tony? No more. *Oopla, bis!* Wine tastes sweet, but an hour in this house, it turns bitter." She paused. "You are not drinking. *L'chaim!*"

Tony drained another poured glass. "L'chaim!"

She clapped her hands, and whirled unsteadily. Tony figured she was tipsy. "Why is this house, a sad house Tony? A house of perpetual woe? Come with me." She gripped his hand and pulled him into a living room cluttered with photos, all of the identical person, a young girl of eighteen years posed in many places, Coney Island, Central Park, school snapshots, walls papered with diplomas and report cards, on the dining table he saw standup photos.

She answered the query in his eyes. "My daughter Miriam, she died in the Triangle Fire. You heard of the fire."

"The East Side still talks about it." Mrs. Hyman said in a ghostly voice. "Still?"

"Happened 20 years ago."

"Happens every day in my house. I live with my daughter! But she is dead! *Oi!* You ask where is my husband? At the shul all day leaving me alone. God forbid you remove one photo! He keeps her alive in this room, but does not see I am dead. Tony! You are Italian, you feel these things, Bernard, my husband is no man to me. Ever since we are not man and wife. I hate him he makes me hate my daughter for what her death did to our marriage. I tear my face, and ask forgiveness! One day I cut my hair to the roots! Bernard resents my presence, our grief was his alone. I lost daughter and husband! What am I to do, Tony? What should I do, look at me, yes, I was broken hearted I cried for a year. Bernard does not realize, he too is dying. What am to do, Tony?" She caressed his hair as in a dumb show. "I am a strong woman, can I help it a passionate woman! Life goes on! Blood runs on, you can't stop it!" She placed his hand on her breasts.

"See Tony how my heart beats, a large heart for suffering, and for love. What must I do Tony, what?" Gripping his hand tightly, she led him to the bedroom. Tony began to feel the rush of the wine to his head. He drew back, her other hand fastened itself on his leg. "How hard!" she said dreamily. She tipped him on to the bed, he was engulfed in Minna's arms, and breasts, who was sobbing and moaning while she seduced him. Her lustiness, and directness left him breathless, after her tears drenched his face.

Later at the door, Minna was shamefaced and shuddering with the expense of tears. She grabbed a shawl from a chair and ran ahead.

"Where are you going?"

"I am going to St. Anne's to pray for forgiveness. Synagogues are closed to women."

"St. Anne's?"

"Yes, I prayed there once. Sadie and Emilia, her best friend, were in each others arms when they jumped from the window."

On Tenth street, Tom reared in front of tenement number 12 where a mob wailed and milled about the stoop, the entrance was clogged. As he forced his entry, a young woman in flapper dress said sadly, "Your ice will become tears today, iceman!"

"Coal today."

"To fire his genius?"

To Tony, it looked like half the Village crowd moved to the East Side. Short flapper skirts, and cloches vied with berets, long scarves partly dragged underfoot, and straw boaters trampled in the gutter. Protests!

"No, no, save him! Sobieski is out of his mind!"

"His face is blue! Has he poisoned himself?"

"Let me through, I must deliver his coal!"

Shouts from the interior, "Grab him! Don't let him on the roof! He will jump!"

"Anton does not need coal, he is going to die on the spot!"

"What is a great pianist without a baby grand? Nothing!"

"How much money among us?"

"Forty-seven dollars!" A man held up a fistful of bills.

"He owes 150 dollars on the Steinway. Not enough! The van is on its way to repossess the piano!"

Tony shouted, "Make way!"

A fiery one turned to him rudely "Shame on you! You are witness to a calamity! Young Anton Sobieski, our virtuoso, is losing his piano to the bourgeois! Losing his life! No consoling! He won't listen. Last night he turned on the gas. Lucky someone sniffed the gas. He's just out of the hospital! But, you are a greenhorn iceman, what do you understand? Nothing! Go back to twirling spaghetti!"

Tony bulled his way up to the second story flat where he saw the pianist, it must have been him, lean and emaciated eyes, ringed black, hair frenzied, clutching a plaster bust of Padereski to his chest.

"Mr Sobieski, I have a coal delivery!"

Sobieski stared at him dumbly, not understanding. "I am Tony, Dominick's son."

He embraced Tony, his clothes smelly of bed sweat. "Ah! Caro Domenico! He heard me play, outside, in the hallway I could hear him clapping and saying 'Bravo, bravo!' Where is Dominick to say bravo again and again, in my misery?"

"He passed away."

"O! The world is dying this day!"

"Who wants your piano?"

"The finance company, any minute the van will be here to take it back, my Steinway! What is to become of my life? I paid up seven hundred dollars, now, for an arrears of 150 dollars it will be repossessed! Go away, these last moments I wish to be alone with my piano!"

Tony spied the baby grand in a corner covered with a Spanish shawl. Tony grabbed Sobieski by the shoulders, and shook him to get his full attention. "Suppose, there is no piano when they come."

"What are you saying?"

"There is no piano—"

The give and take was heard by those thronging the door.

"No piano! Whee! We make the piano disappear? Are you a magician? Bah! Go away."

Someone in the crowd piped, "Listen to him, Anton! He is no magician, but he has a horse and wagon! Do you understand?"

The mob began clapping and whooping, it overflowed the room. Broad laughter became conspiratorial, in sharing a ruse to save the piano. All now crowded around Tony, slapping him on the back, the women hugged him.

"Are you serious?" They clamored for a yes.

"Yes, how many strong backs can I count on?"

"As many as you need!"

Sobieski stood up dazed.

"Don't you get it? The ice man will take away the piano on his ice wagon. Isn't that so ice man?"

"Yes, what time is the van due?"

"In a half hour."

"We have time."

Sobieski was trembled with joyful excitement. "Where will you take it?"

"To my friend, an undertaker, moves a few coffins, and presto there is room in his showroom."

"He is a magician!"

"What are we waiting for? Let's go!"

With a tally-ho twenty men circled the piano, Tony directing them. "Screw off the legs, now, altogether."

The piano was aloft on twenty pair of shoulders and moved carefully down the one flight, and lifted on the wagon. Tony wondered if Jim could pull away, or needed momentum. Sobieski sat on the seat, as Tony egged on the pick up crew to give the wagon a push. The wagon began to roll and headed for Patsy's undertaker parlor. For three months Patsy had the services of Sobieski at the piano playing sad music at the many viewings, not for gratis, Patsy paid him enough so that Sobieski had the balance of the money to pay up. Patsy's daughters got the benefit of free lessons.

His next stop, Svoboda, fifteen cents worth of coal. He was met at the door by two eight year olds, a boy and a girl, identical twins, naked in the draft of the cold hallway. They danced around him, kissing his hands and clapping. Abruptly, distrust appeared in merry eyes, they retreated shrieking to their mother in the kitchen, and clung to her skirt, hiding behind the folds. Mrs. Svoboa a large woman over six feet tall challenged him, her arms folded across her chest

"I am the iceman."

"No, you are not the iceman," she moved towards him truculently.

"I am Tony, Dominick's son."

"Where is Dominick?"

"He is sick."

"A good man. Good man."

"Thank you."

"Leave the coal in the bag near the sink. Or the children will began playing, and blacking themselves." She turned to the children. "You can come out now, he is a nice man, he is Dominick's child."

The children peeked from behind the skirt appearing to be waiting for something.

Mrs. Svoboda pushed them back. "You see, Mr. Tony, your father always brought them candy, so they expect the same from you."

"If I had known. I won't forget next time."

"They were fond of Dominick. Eric and Erika love affection. On Xmas your father always gave presents."

As Tony set down the bag of coal unopened, he saw a mound of paper flowers on the kitchen table. He interrupted homework, half the population of the tenements was engaged in, the twisting together of paper stalks and flowers. Eric and Erika took his hands covered by cold dust and rubbed them against noses to soot them. Then they ran to a full length mirror to look and make funny faces.

"Both are retarded Mr. Tony. My husband left me when they were born, he blamed me. Here is the fifty cents."

"Please, Mrs. Svoboda, buy them something for me, some candy and ice cream."

She pocketed the fifty cents. "You are Dominick's son, you have a good heart." The children scamper around Tony. They needed clothing more than candy. Tony must remind himself to buy underclothing for the children. He would ask Tessie to buy them for his next visit. The twins did not want Tony to leave, holding on to his pants, and whimpering. He placed some soot on his face, they laughed, and he was out the door. Not before Mrs. Svoboda dropped the fifty cent coin in his shirt pocket, and a note to play the lottery, six—seven—nineteen.

Children were raiding the bags of coal scattering coal on the wagon and into the street. It was a short walk to the next stop so he took Tom by the bridle and led him half a block away near Stuyvesant Square, to a modish apartment building. He consulted the blue book, Laetitia Abercrombie: no coal, no ice, no wood kindling. What was he supposed to deliver? And yet there were many entries next to her name, all with no description of delivery. Did she play the lottery? He did not think so. Then why?

A tall, prim looking woman in her thirties was waiting for him on the landing, he thought, or for his father. Her agate blue eyes looked at him questioningly. He doffed his cap. "I am Dominick's son, Tony."

"Where is your father?"

"He is ill three days ago."

"I had not heard."

"It was sudden, Ma'am."

"I shall say a prayer for him."

"Thank you, Ma'am." All the while Tony is wondering why he is standing before this lady's flat with empty hands. She too seemed perplexed.

She recollected herself and the young man before her.

"I am sorry about your father."

"It was sudden, Ma'am."

He entered a spotless apartment that opened on a foyer and a living room. On a chair he saw the starched uniform and cap of a nurse with the name of the Bellevue hospital. "Please sit Mr. Tony, I wish to tell you how much I respected your father." Her skin was very fair, a pert nose slightly freckled, and a lovely smile that radiated her face. She gave off a sense of health. He wished Tessie could look that well even for a day.

There was an embarrassing silence. "Pardon me, but what was it I am supposed to deliver to you, you have central heating and a refrigerator."

She hesitated judging him for a certain trust. "Did your dear father ever speak of me?"

"He was not a talker."

"That is not what I mean. He never mentioned me?"

"No."

"By any chance did he leave a message for me? "I only have his account book, Ma'am."

She stood up and went to the window. She spoke without looking at him. "You are your father's son so I can trust you." Her voice became warm, lilting. She passed her hand through her black bobbed hair, and stood before him. "Yes, messages from the man I love, and he loves me. As you may have noticed, I am a nurse, his surgical nurse. Doctor and I have been in love for the past six years. We wished to marry but his wife will not agree to a divorce.

"I cannot write to him, or phone him because the parents are guarding him from any messages from me. He is now in charge of a department at another hospital uptown so we don't meet as we did in the wards at Bellevue Hospital."

"I gave messages to your father to give to him, and he entrusted messages to him also for me, and your father was the go-between. You must have his name in the book, Henry Nash."

Tony whistled Dr. Nash!

Tony nodded yes.

"It occurred to the doctor to use your father in this way while treating him for an eye infection from cold dust."

"I remember."

"Your father had a good heart, did he love your mother?"

"I think so."

"Your father would not accept any money, so the doctor told him he could be counted on for any medical service."

"Thank you. Will you pass by today and see him."

"I will—I did think of something Ma'am."

"Call me Letty, short for Laetitia."

She extracted a sealed letter from a folder, "Would you please?"

"Yes, I will see him Wednesday to deliver coal."

CHAPTER 5

On the curb he chased a swarm of kids raiding the parked ice wagon for splinters of ice which they sucked like candy pops. A sleepy-eyed man ran into him on the sidewalk, and lingered for an apology. His father warned him against the *habitus* at the cafe. A forehead high on a small head, he wore high-heeled shoes tapping, waiting for an apology.

"You ran into me," said Tony.

"You must always make way for a poet, young man. I am Maurice, the poet."

Tony held on to the bridle, the children made Jim nervous. What would his father do who had great patience? "I did not see you coming, sir."

The poet looked about. "Where is my friend Domenico?"

"He is my father."

"So?"

"He is sick, I am taking his place." Tony noticed he was missing two fingers of his right hand which he used histrionically. He recalled his father saying something about an anarchist poet who lost two fingers while lighting a fuse for a bomb. Innocently, his father had driven Maurice to Union Square where Maurice used the ice wagon as a rostrum for a radical speech. Tony held tight to the bridle trap.

"Your father, I wish him well. One day the ice wagon is a rolling rostrum traveling the world! Your father was patient, he could not drive the wagon through the populace listening to my speech. Are you smiling?"

Tony was not smiling.

"No, you are not. You are Domenico's son. That day, he, and I spoke for the thousands of icemen all over the world who die from arthritis before fifty, or pneumonia, or deathly exhaustion Heroes who ice the sweets and the sorbets, chill the Rothschild wines, shape parfaits, and ice cream effigies of courtiers and capitalists, so that their daughters can cool themselves with frosted fruit. And, you, your children suck on ammoniated ice. You are jellies frozen in place, as the slaves you are. Lend me your ice wagon Domenico's son and onward to Union Square."

"Sir, I have deliveries to make."

"We have messages to deliver! Yes, you are on strike at this moment, we will mobilize all the icemen of the city to strike. Without coal, no ice, they will accede to our demands for a union, and get rid of the gangsters to whom you pay tribute." He began to climb the ice wagon for the seat. Tony stood before him. "If you respect my father Mr. Maurice, you must respect me. I tell you firmly I must go on to finish my rounds. Perhaps we can speak of this matter another day."

Maurice who had one foot on the step-up to the seat backed down. He paused. "You say Domenico is sick?"

"Yes."

"I see there is a necessity for you to carry on. Another time, tomorrow?"

"We'll see."

"The ice wagon shall be my podium, our chariot to run down the carriages of the oppressors." He pinched Tony's cheek, "I have hopes for you, you are well spoken for an iceman's son. That is the future, when an iceman's son will lead the proletariat out of the East Side slums to a new Eden." He saw an empty soda box belonging to the café. He picked it up. Put his fingers to his lips and whispered, "I can stand on this in Union Square," and walked buoyantly in the direction of Union Square.

He heard a shout telling him to move on. The milkman was making a delivery to the cafe. He could not control his horse who sidled up to Jim, they greeted each other with flared nostrils and neighing. Tony felt the sugar cubes in his pocket his father gave him. He palmed them to both horses while the milkman scowled on his buckboard seat.

Tony was behind time in his deliveries, he rushed Jim, and himself, the rest of the day. He passed by the undertaker establishment of Patsy Paglieri, its somber, stained glass front, the mahogany trim, and a brass plate The portly figure of Patsy waved to him while hiking his gold watch chain higher on his chest and holding aloft not a *Toscano*, but a Cuban cigar. His bent fingers showed off gold rings, four this afternoon. He was told that arthritis was cured in the presence of gold. His torso was barreled on dwarfish legs. He could turn on a face with the affability of a benevolent uncle, or it became one of soulful gravity, depending on the means, and the quality of the deceased. He was the neighborhood fixer of traffic tickets, subpoenas, eviction notices, and a bag man for police, and politicians. Proudly, he stood in front of his funeral parlor, a Charon waiting for his next fare. Patsy was not smiling. Did he know? Did it happen? Tony became panicked, was his father dead, had Patsy got the word already? He cancelled two deliveries without a second look, allowed Jim to find his way back to the stable, and ran on foot to his tenement. His stomach ached with nervous spasms. That bastard Patsy is in a hurry to bury his father! He leaped the stairs to the fifth floor and burst into the flat bumping into Tessie, who was dressed in black. His legs gave way, he fell to the linoleum floor, banging his fists against it. "No! No! Papa! No!"

Tessie helped him up, he leaned against her, he could smell the fragrance of withered flowers on that same dress she wore for their mother's funeral.

"Where, Tessie?"

"In his room. I contacted Mr. Paglieri."

"How can you be so cool."

"He died peacefully."

Tony sat beside the body of Dominick until Patsy Paglieri arrived. His father looked so shriveled, his skin blanched yellow as if vinegared by age and toil. A cheap print of a Madonna and Child on tin backing hung above the bedstead. Clasped hands on his bony sternum held Tessie's rosary, and missal. He would lie in that bed during the wake, one chest, and one chair would be moved to make room for a kneeling stool, and flowers. He must mend a shade to blacken the bedroom which will be candlelit. He lay by his father on the bed, unclasping his hands to join with his. This is what Patsy Paglieri saw when he entered the room. His saddened face was his condolence greeting, equal for all, except those of quality.

Tony locked the door of the bedroom, he wanted last hours with his father to talk. What about? What made immigrant fathers so closemouthed? Dominick never shared a dream, a ricordo of the old country, of his youth, did he love his wife, a joke he heard, did he covet cuts of meat he could not afford for the Sunday *ragu*, why didn't they cry these old men, did Dominick actually cry and confide to old Jim in the privacy of the stable? Why didn't he hug me, as I am hugging him. Yes, he loved me in his own way, in his taciturn manner. Was it the impoverished crisscross of language that no wine could bridge between father and son? Nonetheless, Tony spoke to him, told him how that morning he used his shaving brush and razor proudly. Teresa sat at the kitchen table with Patsy to make arrangements She ordered a hearse, and two limousines which had just been delivered to Patsy to replace coach and horse, although the bereaved considered the carriages and black plumed horses more regal, like a state funeral. She gave Patsy the cemetery deed which allowed for one more burial in a twin grave at Fourth Calvary. Patsy wore gray gloves and a black tie as sympathetic gestures. A fee for opening the grave, the cost of a modest coffin of walnut wood, embalming, amounted to four hundred and fifty dollars. With two hundred and forty-five dollars at Dime Savings, a balance of two hundred and fifteen dollars was owed to Mr. Paglieri. He trusted them for the balance.

"Can I speak to Tony?"

"Not now, Mr. Paglieri."

"We need the body for embalming. I come tonight. Where is the viewing?"

"In the bedroom, the living room is too small."

"I'll see Pastor Keenan on my way back to the office to arrange for a Mass at St. Anne's."

CHAPTER 6

Early April, the winding five flights to the bier-bed of Domenico Di Napoli was suffocating by sweating bodies of workmen and working women, and housewives who were paying last respects. Father John Keenan who was forced to high jump over the bodies of the mourners to arrive at the bed-bier to say final prayers before the next day's funeral mass at St. Anne's saw many of his parish tiered along the yellow marble steps. Children of the East Siders were down below playing box ball, or handing out bleeding noses to each other. As they queued up the steps the mourners were hosted on the landings by the tenants of that flight, Slovaks, German, Jewish, Poles, who proffered a drink of water, hot chicken soup, a fruit, cookies, a shot of *rosolio* liqueur, a commiserating sigh and a sorrowful nod. The flat steamed with the press of people in close quarters and the withering away of five or six wreaths of flowers pillowing Domenico. The drying leaves and blooms became frayed, powered, and caused many to sneeze and cough. The largest wreath was signed Laetitia Abercrombie and Dr. Henry Nash. Teresa retreated to the kitchen that looked out on an airway between tenements. The window of the bedroom was shut tight to keep out the teeth-rattling tremor of the tracks, the squeal of steel upon steel.

Patsy Paglieri, the undertaker, in his black cutaway ushered the viewers in and out of the flat. Tony stood at the head of the bed in his best Sunday clothes, except for his father's vest on which dangled Domenico's gold-plated Elgin watch. He stood there immobile like a funerary figure of stone until Patsy roused him with a cup of bitter coffee brewing on the flat top of the stove all day which added to the steaminess of the flat. Patsy helped himself to the last bottle of *rosolio* distilled by Domenico from an extract of *mandarino*.

"Where is Teresa? Get her out into the air."

"In the kitchen open window near air shaft."

"How about the roof?"

"Still snow on the roof. Teresa breathe good in kitchen."

Patsy scurried to the front of the mourners and kneeled to welcome the priest. Father Keenan, pastor of St. Annes was present to say farewell prayers in the intimacy of the home. First, he expressed his condolences to Tony, new master of the home. Patsy handed him a short glass of *rosolio*. Father Keenan fingered it while speaking to Tony.

"I wish it were under different circumstances that we meet Anthony, Teresa has spoken so often of you during Sodality meetings, how brilliant you are."

"Older sisters, Father Keenan, are not trustworthy about younger brothers."

"On the contrary, I heard the same from other sources. You are always hitting the books."

"I am on the math team, it is competitive with other schools, so we must maintain a sharp edge."

"Sharp indeed, Anthony, I must confess I was tempted to ask Teresa to persuade you to enroll at Fordham so you could join the math team, and win the nationwide scholastic competition."

"It's my last year, Father."

"But you see I was not up to the deviousness. When you graduate, lend a mind to attend Villanova. I did my undergraduate work there, who would believe it twenty five years ago."

"Not this year, Father."

"Whenever, Anthony. I seldom see you in church. I assume you are a scoffing mathematician, a young skeptic. Perhaps, that is why some months ago your sister, Teresa, asked me if there was a patron saint of numbers, a medallion of that saint might bring you back to the church who also welcomes men of learning. I did not know that saint. I asked Sister Clothilde to find out, and she did." Father Keenan held up a medallion on a chain bright as gold.

"Father, thank you, that was another time. We cannot afford it now."

Father Keenan grinned good-naturedly, "Of course, the medallion is bait to sit you in a pew of St. Anne's. Accept it as a gift from me, not entirely innocent, I gamble on the medallion's efficacy. It is our Saint Albertus Magnus, mathematician."

"But, it is gold, Father."

"Not quite, Anthony, only plated. Will do no harm. No claims. A sign of our friendship." Patsy off to the side, within earshot, is signaling to Anthony to accept the gift.

"Thank you, father, you are very kind."

He placed the chained medallion round Tony's neck. "To our friendship," Father made a sweep of his right arm. "I see you are left-handed, I am right-handed, perfect partners on a handball court. You have the makings of a strong player."

"Only box ball, Father."

"That's a beginning. When you are free, meet me at the Boy's Club on Tompkin's Square where we can hustle on the court." Viewers were restless, Pastor Keenan was suddenly solemn to lead the prayer of the dead.

Patsy is signaling again to kiss the hand of the next Monsignor. Tony bowed slightly, and joined the prayer.

While the priest was intoning the prayer, Sister Clothilde, and Teresa were kneeling on the kitchen floor near an open window. She, and Teresa, were not really friends because of eight years difference in age, and her vocation. They saw each other frequently at the sodality meetings, and a drive for funds to build a playground for the children. They shared common ground in the appreciation of the religious poetry of Christina Rossetti. Often in the choir loft, Sister Clothilde expressed her concern that Teresa did not go on to college after high school. She passed two entrance exams. Teresa explained time, and again, her family could not afford two in higher education. An unbearable strain on family budget. Finally, Sister Clothilde pressed no more, realizing well there was a bountiful grace in self-sacrifice. They were a contrast. Teresa always appeared in blooming health except for the feverish eyes. Sister Clothilde's face had an enigmatic aspect, and morbidly beautiful, with a brooding brow, shadowed, gray penitential eyes, over all, a somber beauty. Her complexion was darker than Teresa's, that French darkness, for she was of French-Canadian origin, born on a lonely farm on one of the scattered island of the Maritimes. Her name was Denise Duval. The prayer was over. They were standing when Patsy entered with another bottle of *rosolio* with two shot glasses. Both accepted the *rosolio*, Teresa winced when she drank it, Sister Clothilde drank it slowly, tastefully.

Pastor Keenan offered a simple eulogy to a half empty church. Dominick was an honest, hardworking ice man who was always prompt in his coal deliveries to the rectory and, he was told by parishioners, to whom Dominick sold coal, that he would never substitute bituminous coal for anthracite, for soft bituminous smoke could suffocate people in close quarters. His daughter Teresa is a member of the sodality, and his son Anthony was baptized, received communion, and confirmation at St. Anne's. God bless his soul, Amen! What would the poet Maurice have said from the pulpit: Dominick Di Napoli was a noble iceman!

Back from the burial, Tony offered Mr. Paglieri his father's Elgin watch and Teresa added her mother's gold wedding ring. He said he could wait, and thanked them. When Tony checked the stable, old Jim was dead in his stall. Tony made a wreath of straw and laid it on his hoary head. He phoned the sanitation department to send around the pick up van for dead animals. He stood by until it arrived, and it did. Often, a day or two elapsed, and the swollen horse becomes prey for stray dogs and carrion flies. He took off his hat as the pulley of the van drew Jim into the interior with other dead.

That evening, he sat down with Teresa to figure what to do tomorrow and the next day.—First thing, he must buy a horse, he could not afford a flivver truck. Then, Tony could see if he could enlarge his route to increase the income. They could always pawn the watch and the ring. The coldwater flat still reeked of the sickish smell of faded wreaths that were laid at the foot of the bed, there was no bier. It caused Tony to sneeze.

"Gee, sis, open a window." He remembered her cough. "Never mind!"

"Don't baby me like Papa did! At the wake, my girl friend Laura, who works at the Henry Street Settlement House as a cook says they need a translator for the Italian immigrants, and the children. I speak enough Italian to be understood which I studied on my own. It is not a shirt waist factory."

"I say no."

"This way we can save enough money so you can go back to school. I am of age, what must I do all day around the house with Papa gone? When he was here, I washed, I cooked, and took care of him."

"Well, try it sis, but not before you go for a check up and get a go ahead from Dr. Nash at the clinic."

"I am going to do just that! I will go to clinic on Wednesday, when Dr. Nash is there."

"Do I deserve a kiss?"

"Not one, but two. In all the confusion of the wake, I misplaced a library book."

"What is the title?"

"It's poetry."

He teased, "Love poetry?"

"You stick to your math Tony. You may find an equation for love."

"Well, well—"

Tony headed for Patsy Paglieri's office to see if he had a horse for sale. He was now using long bodied Lincoln limousines for funerals. Patsy led him to a one-eyed horse. "Name is Tom, first horse. No put him down, others to glue factory."

"Thanks. Patsy, I owe you again."

"Owe? Who know when I ask you for favor, eh?"

"Ask, Patsy."

"Maybe, sometime, eh, Tony."

CHAPTER 7

Teresa saw Dr. Nash at the clinic as promised to Tony. He ordered X-rays and a battery of tests. He will get in touch with her about the results. In the meantime, she should rest, and avoid crowds. She was running a low, intermittent fever. She was home bound until she heard from him. An April sun, and a soft breeze lured her to the fire escape, there was a view of the arrowed length of Fourteenth Street. Long ago, Teresa sloughed off Domenico's fear of white slavers who kidnapped nubile girls to force them into brothels. A great part of the population of New York once lived in furnished rooms to accommodate hordes of single boarder immigrants. A popular way to earn extra income was the rental of a room, or two, in a flat. When he made his drops in the kitchens, Domenico was crisscrossed by men warming themselves by the stove, or filling a glass of iced water. All appeared as from a warren. When Tony tethered his horse on Fourteenth Street, he was in the midway of a teeming metropolis buzzing with activity from the East River to Union Square. A commercial midway for plain and bizarre restaurants, burlesque took over legitimate theatres to while away the hours of unemployed men, one heard *balalaikas* from Russian cafes, the spectacles of Academy of Music, its top hat opera goers, Luchow's, redolent of German beer in morning cleanups, the sepulcher white Child's pancakes in window display on griddles, the ingenious ring of coin bins of the Automat, sleepy-eyed cooks entering Tony Pastor's, Irving Theatre at Irving Place now tawdry, the Player's club at Gramercy Square, the promenade of streetwalkers in frowzy dress, newsboys sleeping in hallways, or hawking editions under puny arms. Every edition was an extra, extra!—the yellow Graphic, the close printed Sun, the stately Herald Tribune, the brash News, the Mirror, the Journal American, Pulitzer's World, until the street spread grandly into spacious Union Square where anarchists, communists, socialists, and sheer troublemakers staked claims for soapbox oratory. How so and so's little girl who is in the hospital with rheumatic fever? Teresa recalled with a shudder, in March, one quarter of her class did not rejoin the class, as they reached puberty, they died of damaged hearts. Did Gennaro's wife have a baby, was there a dragnet of drunks and bums on the street? Did Tony forget to tell Ms. Svoboda to have her twins vaccinated? Did the Health Department warn all infant mothers to heat the milk from open milk cans to avoid scrofula from tubercular cows? Was the Vice Society patrolling the Red Light street? She heard La Traviata was billed at the Academy, the Con Edison building will be enlarged, the New York Telephone Company is hiring immigrant girls as operators, the Henry Street Settlement has added visiting nurses, St. Anne's has staged a drive for a playground for the Catholic Elementary school, Luther Adler will emote a first Jewish King Lear at the Thalia Theatre, Giovanni Grasso, and Mimi Aguglia will be performing at the People's Theatre in the Fall, Eva La Galliene has begun a Repertory Theatre, Russeks is holding a sale on mink and beaver furs, Hearns opened a toy department—

"What's new, Tony?"

Tony spared her the incident of Vincenzo and the bull.

One of the first customers of Domenico was the pastry and bakery shop on Bayard Street owned by Vincenzo Vitale, who was now in his late seventies. He still confected the finest *sfogliatelle* anywhere, that unique Neapolitan pastry of coiled strands filled with almond cream. Although the sore was ill-kept by his aged wife, it still thrived.

People traveled distance after they moved from the East Side for the tastiness of the <u>sfogliatelle</u> of Vincenzo in limited supply because of his years. Tony was always amazed as a child to see incomparable *sfoglia* baked crisply to perfection issuing from an antiquated coal-fired oven, pitted and crumbling, an opening like the maw of a toothless hag. And lying about were bags of sugar and flour carelessly spilled to an earthen floor, gallons of opened orange water, cans of almond paste, and segmented citron. When with his father, Vincenzo gave him a hot *sfogliatelle* from the oven and Tony ate it all gingerly. And the fruity, alcoholic essences of the confectioner's flavors made him heady. Not this morning at 4 a.m., he was standing on the last chipped steps leading down deeply into the grotto-like bakery shouldering two large bags of coal. As he pushed upon the door a draft, an odd flavor filled his nostrils. Blood. The bakery was a shambles of bloodied bags of flour and sugar, some rent, spilled and littered with torn bodies of huge, gray tenement rats, a few still alive glaring with red rodent eyes, and foaming at the jaws. Tony dropped the coal when he saw old Vincenzo cornered by a bulldog terrier who was capable of slaughtering the old man, as he had slaughtered the rats. Poor Vincenzo was quaking before a tier of baking pans, the carnage stained bulldog was snarling and darting as Vincenzo warded off the kill crazed terrier with an oven paddle. Tony leaped back to the sidewalk, seized the three pronged steel ice shaver from the wagon, and descended, clanging the steel shaver on the concrete steps to divert the dog from Vincenzo. The terrier wheeled, saw him, and charged. Tony impaled him by the throat with the shaver, and pinned him to the earth where he quivered, and expired. Vincenzo collapsed in his arms. After his fright, Vincenzo told Tony he hired the bull dog from a pet shop under the Third Avenue L. He was told the American bull terrier was often deployed to rid premises of tenement rats. Cats were slain and eaten by oversized river rats.

At suppertime, Teresa asked, "What's new, brother?"

Should he tattle about her doctor's illicit affair with Miss Abercrombie? His father never spilled the beans. Besides, Teresa wasn't one for gossipy titillations.

"Well, two police commanders were indicted for accepting bribes from brothels along Fourteenth Street. Did you hear Prosperity is Around the Corner, the stock market is rebounding, Al Smith is sponsoring an outing for the democratic clubs at Ulmer Park next Saturday."

"Are we going?"

"I got an invite from the ward captain."

"I love the outings, the sea, the fresh air! What else is new?"

"The Brooklyn Dodgers have a chance at the pennant this year."

"Boo! We are Giant fans, aren't we?"

"They say Ziegfield Follies is bankrupt. Mary Pickford and Douglas Fairbanks are in England, Ford will not fire anyone in these bad times, the Roxy Theatre will be the biggest in the world, there will be baby parade at Mardi Gras in Coney Island, Luna Park's bathing beauties got offers from Mack Sennett, New York Hospital is moving uptown, Booth Memorial Hospital is a woman's hospital, Klein's, and Ohrbach's are having clearance sales."

"I'll buy an outfit at Ohrbach's for Ulmer Park."

"Don't tell me you are going to buy, you get cold feet, every item on the racks is too expensive, and you come home with nothing?"

Teresa bought a becoming dress, and matching shoes, and joined the women of the ward sitting on milk wagons, ice wagons, bakery wagons, all festooned with paper streamers. Chevrolet, Star, Willys-Knight, Hupmobile, chain driven Macks, a Stutz Bearcat, and Ford flivvers led the caravan to Cropsey Avenue and Ulmer Park on Gravesend Bay. Behind them trekked complimentary kegs of beer on Bulldog trucks, and hauling wagons further furbelowed by American flags supplied by politicos. Children of all sizes swarmed like ants over everything in sight on the picnic grounds of Ulmer Park. A mass picnic. A caravanserai, where the national foods were cooked as in one large stew pot. The Melting Pot! Poles, Jews, Italians, Germans, Bohemians, etc. Each had an assigned zone equipped with outdoor grills from which steamed or smoked, aromas of cabbage, sausage, simmering *ragu* sauce, frankfurters, bratwurst, pastrami, corned beef, perogies, blintzes, borscht—and also the mixed merriment of dance, jigging, mazurkas, polkas, tarantellas—until the starry sky shined as in a chandeliered ballroom. They lingered, urging bunioned feet to one more dance, dragging themselves back to the cold water flats, reluctant to leave the dew-tipped green grass and the freshening evening breeze off Shore Road. On these outings, Teresa was out front, at the end of the jetty, or collecting shells on the pebbly shore, playing tag with the curling surf, gathering lost children, declaiming poetry aloud in the setting sun. Where was Tony? Under the shadow of a black thorn tree cracking a new math text!

At one of the outings in June on Teresa's 18th birthday. the young crowd could not resist the lure of nearby Coney Island, the song driven shoreward by the breezes on that Atlantic beach, the roaring swoop of the roller coasters tailed by screams, the wavering tones of the calliopes playing On the Sidewalks of New York at the caprice of gusts, the clanking of mechanical rides, and the hum of a million human voices gamboling on the beaches, the humming hive of amusement Parks, and dancing fox trots in the dancehalls. While the oldsters. drowsed on full bellies of beer and more beer, the young people sneaked off to the Playground of the World, a half mile away from Ulmer Park The girls made straight for the huge dancehall of Luna Park. On its burnished parquet floor Teresa led a rejecting little brother who lumbered along in a fox trot until dramatically a swarm of sailors appeared and partnered the squealing girls. If one stood tiptoe, a United States cruiser was in harbor view. A redheaded gob swept Teresa on to the center of the floor, both danced so well together, others made room for them. Tony sat gladly on the sidelines amazed, open mouthed at the dancing ability of his sister. He never realized she had a pretty figure as she danced with all her might the waltz, foxtrot, the Lindy, the Peabody—He wondered where she learned all the dance steps, he figured she and girl friends practiced on the roof of the tenement on cool days when high laced shoes would not stick in sun heated tar. Round, and round, Teresa, and the sailor tripped the light fantastic while Tony watched the Chute of Chutes where boats from a height splashed into an artificial lagoon before the Tower of Lights. As the sun dipped, like the loss of Cinderella's slipper, it signaled the end of the escapade. Minarets began to flicker, and glow in the gathering dusk. The girls parted from the sailors with reluctant hugs and goodbyes. He saw his sister exchanging addresses with the sailor who held a stubby pencil He never saw her so vivacious, at the moment, he was jealous of the gob who made such a spark with Teresa. For the next three days back in the flat, Teresa walked about as in a dream. His inkwell was dry, pages were missing from his note pads, the nibs of his pens were worn, and she borrowed part of his allowance to buy stamps. This one way correspondence went on for a month, only silence at the other end. Teresa moped for a time Tony heard the cruiser was on a world wide cruise and would not be back to the homeport for a year. He endured silently Teresa's sighing and mooning on the roof when the breezes were soft from the East River. Tony was patient with his once enchanted sister. She perked up suddenly a Sunday afternoon after Mass at St. Anne's. He could tell because she gave him a big, lasting hug. And, Tony regained the end of the kitchen table on which he did his school assignments.

After his rounds, "What's new Tony?"

He spared her the tragedy, his delivery to Mrs. Rutherford Moorehead in the mansion row on East Twelfth, the homestead of her father, Brigadier General Thomas Moorehead of the Union Army. A stop, he never shared with his father. The mansion had a Greco Roman facade, imperial in style, it shared the street elbowed to other mansions. He consulted the route book of his father, it diagramed crudely the arrangement of the rooms. The mansion was subdivided into ten rooms let out to single persons, which was done to defray the upkeep of the patrician possession. The book noted: carry a sixty pound block of ice just beyond an umbrella rack and clothing closet, there ice pick the allotted chunks of ice for ten rooms with small fridges. There was no mark that the second floor cocooned the privacy of the Moorehead family. As you left the umbrella rack, you entered a marble colonnade of four piers upholding a faux Arcadian arbor of stuccoed acanthus leaves, a pace ahead an atrium. A Civil War Caesar! On the walls hung swords, scabbards, battalion flags, and daguerreotypes of men in blue uniform. He took a stairway on his right and knocked on a door on the second floor.

A soft voice replied, "Please, do enter."

When he did, he saw at the end of an enormous room, a large canopied bed, ornately carved. On a high bed lay a person up to her chin in a coverlet although it was the month of June. As the person slid out of bed, her bare feet dangled. Tony saw the figure of a young woman in a flannel nightgown and night cap. The blinds were half closed. She pattered up to him in puffy slippers, and stared, puzzled, pushed back her nightcap, her head was patchy with stray locks. An unpleasant odor exuded from her body. She leaned weakly against his chest exclaiming, "Take me with you! I am a prisoner." When she peeked up at him pleadingly, he saw a ravaged face of pustules, her eyes were colorless, mewing sounds as from a kitten issued from grey lips. Her neckline was caked with scaly sores, and blue lesions. He looked up to a coffered ceiling to conceal his aversion. Abruptly, she stepped back to smooth her straggled hair and smiled coquettishly. Her teeth were brittle white like soft chalk.

"Have you come to court me? My mother said Mr. Clarence Crawford would call."

Tony felt a sharp dig in his ribs, he turned to encounter Mrs. Moorehead, a tall, angular woman in a morning attire of severe colored cloth.

Coldly she asked, "What are you doing here?" Did she have to ask? A chunk of ice was melting on the parquet floor, his tongs beside his foot.

"Sorry, Ma'am, I mistook the room."

"Well, leave and find the rented rooms to deliver your ice. Where is Signor Dominick?"

"I am his son, he passed away."

"Quel *dommage*."

"Mother, you are mistaken, this is Mr. Clarence Crawford, you said he was calling on me soon. He evidently forgot to leave his calling card."

"Hush child."

She placed her arm about her daughter's shoulders, led her back to bed, and covered her with the coverlet.

"As you see, my only daughter Cornelia, mistook you for a gentleman caller."

"I hope she feels better, Ma'am."

She looked at him long. "You remind me of an innocent time, of a young promising man of New York blood who danced with her at her debut." She saw the puddle of ice on the floor. Tony wiped it dry with his kerchief.

"I am sorry, iceman, what were you saying?"

"I hope your daughter feels better."

"Thank you. Now finish your business."

Cornelia waved to him from under the coverlet.

After Tony serviced the warren of rooms, he brushed past an elderly man who was sweeping the front walk Tony apologized.

"Don't blame you in a hurry to get out."

"I am Tony, the iceman."

"You are Dominick's son, he spoke of you often, he was proud of you."

"He never told me about the second floor or left instructions."

"I am what they once called, a family retainer, a fancy servant. Now, my staff is a broom."

"I left a puddle on her floor."

"I'll take care of the puddle."

"Thank you kindly."

Tony looked up at Cornelia's window framed by sculptured garlands.

"So you strayed to the second floor. You saw the young miss?"

"Yes."

"Was Mrs. Rutherford cross with you."

"I thought so," said Tony.

"You can't blame the poor woman. Cornelia eloped with a ne'er do well chauffeur three years ago. He abandoned her. She returned home last August very ill, that morbid disease syphilis, a death that will end in madness."

"Is that what it looks like?"

"She was the prettiest debutante at the ball at the Waldorf."

"Why don't they open a window in her bedroom?"

"She has no immunity from colds."

The thought of Teresa flashed through his mind and the forever, closing windows.

"Don't breathe a word to anyone about poor Cornelia."

And Tony did not tell Teresa about meeting Cornelia.

"What's new, Tony?"

Patsy needed help with burials, infants were dying by the hundreds on the East Side of diarrhea and tubercular milk. Every tenement door was tagged with tiny nosegays of budding white flowers to announce a baby death. Wailing and keening in the hallways Tony found unbearable. The East Side was awash with tears for innocent dead children. When families could not pay for a tiny casket, Patsy cushioned fancy fruit baskets with cheap satin and buried them in multiple graves.

Friday, the end of Tony's first week solo on Dominick Di Napoili's ice wagon, time for a bath at the Municipal Bathhouse. He counted on more than twenty minutes to shower, to get rid of his sweat, the muzzle froth of the horse, the grime and powder of the dirty streets, and the fibers of manure between toes. Too, he imagined he reeked of semen. Although, he sponged down in cold water before leaving in the morning, nothing like the shower cleansing that made him feel newly baptized. Teresa accompanied him before today, the Municipal Bathhouse was proscribed by Dr, Nash until he had an answer to her intermittent fevers and coughing. Tony carried messages for her friends, Angie, Nanina, Josephine, Rosie, Laura, Leah, in return she was eager for gossip of the latest courting among the singles of the neighborhood. Her friends did not visit lately, wary of the white plague, tuberculosis. That suspicious cough was all too familiar. That winter, in one tenement, more than twenty tenants were ravaged fatally by TB. The granite stoop was ankle deep of fallen, withered flowers from funeral corsages pinned on the plain board doors. Under Tammany's control the bathhouses were the richest source of building graft in the city. Money poured into the design of the bathhouses located in the fetid ghettoes of immigrants. The bathhouses resembled Greek temples, all architectural gems, as politicians siphoned off enormous graft that could have been used to regulate the installment of interior bathrooms and running water in the cold flats. It was the bathers only experience of grandeur. For years the bathhouses were shut down, until the Depression, when they were restored to use by the Works Project Administration of the New Deal. The bathhouse was cavernous, humid and steamy as Tony paid ten cents for the loan of a towel and a bar of soap courtesy of Colgate and Co. He was given a number, when called he undressed in a shared locker room, stored his clothing in a closet, then entered an area of a hundred showers whose temperature was controlled by an employee who allowed you twenty minutes to soap, and shower, then you squeezed by backto locker to towel yourself. After you dressed, you jammed the newly washed in a thronged lobby for social exchanges with neighbors. A chatter of many tongues rose to the vaulted ceiling as if seeking a resounding board for perfect intonation-The Melting Pot.

By the entrance door, in a small alcove to the right, a Friday regular was, what the manager of the baths kindly called, the house artist. The manager provided a chlorine bleached table on which rested an easel 9 by 6 inches. supporting a sketch pad. The artists right arm was limp at his side, so he sketched with his left hand pen and ink head studies as the bathers posed one after another, some had been portrayed before but they were flattered by the attention of the artist. He was Casimir, Kodaly, illustrator for a socialist print in the United States. His limp arm was the mayhem of strike breakers in Pittsburgh where he was assigned to render a pictorial report of a bitter strike. At the time, he drew and painted with his right hand, he learned to use his left equally well. At first glance, he was an employee of the bathhouse, his attire matched, same workman shoes, heavy twill trousers, a woolen shirt, a miner's cap, a souvenir of Pittsburgh. Instead of a belt, he used a knotted rope reminding Tony of church paintings of ascetic friars. Since his return from the maiming in Pittsburgh, he was seated at that desk every Friday doing sketch portraits of the bathers. Never a fee, or a price. He was grateful that they permitted themselves to pose no more than ten minutes. When he finished a sketch, he set it aside in a pile, and no amount of prompting, cajoling, or price, was it available to the sitter. Why he piled up sketched portraits one upon another to take them home in a large portfolio was a mystery to all the sitters. Tony never posed, or wished to, unlike Teresa and her companions, so Tony was surprised when the artist addressed him in acoarse voice.

"Where is your sister, young man?"

"My sister? Oh! She is not feeling well" sir."

"I am sorry, tell her I was asking after her."

"I will, sir."

Tony had never been so close to the artist. He was about fifty years of age, his skin was the color of dried blood, his eyes were darkly patched, thick grey hair was tousled by the frequent nervous sweep of his sketching hands which marked his forehead with streaked ink, the eyes of a gentle confessor. About him a strange odor like rotted hay, his fingers were yellowed by stains of smoking, which probably coarsened his voice, so contrary, if compared to his gentle blue eyes.

"During the sitting some months ago, she spoke of you in high terms, you are a math prodigy"

"You know how sisters are, sir."

'Would you pose for a sketch?"

"No, thank you."

"Why not, I have sketched many who have had an ear or two nicked by river rats"

Tony touched the lobe of his left ear where a rat wedged a cut, now a noticeable slit, the size of a thin pencil.

"Don't be embarrassed Tony. A cleft lobe is the badge of the tenements."

Tony had forgotten the slight disfigurement. So common, no one felt branded. Anyway, Tony was a bit ticked off by the artist's personal remark. "What's the purpose of the sketches, the sitters never possess them, you do everyone, and take them to your studio, No one knows what you do with them."

Casimir gave a dry chuckle. "I have no such amenity as a studio. I won't harp on a sitting, I do insist that you accompany me home, I shall tell you what I do with the portraits. You are a smart ass, yes, I like that. If I confessed here, who would listen or understand Casimir's project. It will be a secret. between us Aren't you flattered you have been chosen. If I were younger I would claim you as a brother confidant. Artists, as you see, are poor but rich in intuition."

That instant resentment of the ear nick passed, Tony felt a sudden sympathy for the man. Then, wouldn't Teresa be thrilled if he solved the mysterious purposes of the portraits. He was going back home empty handed of gossip for Teresa. A revelation would please her, and distract her from worrying about Dr. Nash's coming report.

"I live two blocks away, you wonder why I keep the sketches, thousands? Come, I'll tell you why, I need to."

Tony was persuaded too, by the artist's abject appeal. He nodded yes. Tony relieved the painter of the weight of the accumulated sketches When Casimir stood up, he towered over Tony, although there was a marked stoop in his carriage. It was the first week of April with the last cold bite of March in the air. The sky was starry between the looming tenements. Only a short walk to the artist's ground floor flat on St. Mark's Square. The flat contained two large rooms, the parlor room was a beaver's mound of canvases, sketches, rickety easels, and books strewn half-opened. In one corner, stood a collection of Byzantine styled oils. A kitchen stove separated the outer room from the inner where prominently alone, stood a teak wood bed of oriental decoration, a four poster tented by discolored red silk, the sides enclosed by the same cloth. Pillowed solely, with no mattress. Casimir Kodaly cleared a stool of tubes of paint and asked Tony to be seated. That first scent of what seemed to be clotted, and rotted hay inhabited the room and surrounded the curious bed. The walls displayed many oils, watercolors, all sketches of persons in attitudes of sleeping, of all ages. A rack of Chinese design held a number of long stemmed pipes, and a Bunsen burner beneath a clay bowl. Casimir gave Tony a chance to absorb what he saw. He busied brewing a pot of tea with an eye on Tony to judge his response to the scene. He hoped Tony would ask, and he did.

"Sir, why so many sleeping people,"

"They fill me with tenderness as I gaze on them, they are dreaming. Half our lives are dreaming. May I call you Tony, you may call me Casimir, Casimir Kodaly. Sit Tony, let me explain too, why I sketch our folk of the East Side?" Tony sat on a high ottoman that tipped.

"When I sketch in the bathhouse I am collecting faces to eventually paint one iconic figure, or face, if you will, who will be the quintessential soul of the sitters, of the immigrant poor, who find the only pleasure in deeply satisfying dreams. What can we imagine in those dreams? All the hopes, freedom, a fantasy life compared to the brutal reality of daily conscious existence as benighted humans. What I tryto capture is the imago, the image, the icon of this humanity, of the ghettoes. Do you follow me, Tony?

"Yes, sir.

'Did you know Da Vinci's paintings are mathematical compositions, although sensuous?"

"I don't."

Casimir opened a closet, from it fluttered the portraits.

"Where among them is that icon to represent the dream life of the New York ghetto dwellers?"

Tony was about to blurt: Teresa! He bit his lip shut.

"I lost my right arms for a cause. I planned to kill myself. I taught my left hand to restore my art."

"I am sorry."

"I noticed you sniffing when you entered this room. It is opium Tony, opium. There are my pipes, I am overdue for a smoke" He picked up a pipe and began to stuff the bowl with a gummy substance then laid the pipe back on the rack. "I have been a socialist all my life to bring to humbled humanity a better life. But who can rescue them from suffering, from relentless aging, disillusion, drabness and desolation of spirit." He tapped the pipe rack. "This is my surcease. How I wish I could envelope the East Side in a cloud of opium to give them unimaginably lovely dreams, a sense of time which feels eternal, all images in colors to rival sunsets, visions of palaces and beautiful gardens, and not the squatting tenements, the Arab word for a garden is paradise. Why not give them this milk of paradise, opium? The milk of paradise on earth! To give them epiphanous beauty they will never experience on earth. I unburden myself to you. You are a sensitive young man. My sketches at the bathhouse are only exercises now, I have given up ambition to capture in a face that psyche, the flesh and blood of this ghetto. Rather, I would give them that milk of paradise and invite them to dream the glory dreams of that vegetable God who is immanent in opium."

"Are you offering me opium?

"You are too young to have character. When you grow into character, you will begin to suffer, and maybe share a pipe, or two with me"

The tea was cold. The artist was suddenly fatigued. "Tony, thank you for coming, as you see I am tired, I have spoken too long and not well at all, forgive me if what I say is odd to your ears. Thank you for carrying the sketches, and my regards to your sister." Casimir reached for his pipe and began to light it with a taper.

Tony was in a daze as he hit the street. His thoughts were as gummed up as that opium glob in the artist's pipe at this moment, without the benefit of a dream, When Teresa called out from the bedroom:

"Did you see the girls?"

"No, they went to a dance at Webster Hall."

"Oh!"

Tony could not sleep, his mind was racing with the confession of the artist. Why Tony? He seldom smoked. He grabbed one of his father's *Toscanos* and went up to the roof to smoke, to think. The ghetto was asleep under a gibbous moon directly overhead, the flat roofs were stepping stones to the East River, dirty brick was maculated by patches of moonlight, a large cloud illumined by the moon lay low like a blanket, or a comforter, upon the slumber of thousands of sleepers. He drew deeply on the cigar, and flicked the gray ashes. If that cloud were Casimir's cloud of opium, would the anguish of existence be assuaged by the milk of paradise? What teased Tony, and kept Tony wide awake was Casimir's remark that mathematics could be sensuous! A sensuous equation? He flicked the cigar into the depths of an airway. In two hours, he was due at the stable to begin his rounds He entered Teresa's room and tucked the covers.

"What's new."

That was the refrain each day addressed to Tony until she heard from Dr. Nash about the tests. Then, free from her isolation! What will he eventful tomorrow? What's new?

CHAPTER 8

Dr. Henry Nash was born of a long line of Episcopalian ministers who officiated at Trinity church. Early, he prepared for the ministry, midway he heard another claim, that of medicine. He was now Chief of Pulmonology at Bellevue. He was 45 years of age, married to a socialite woman. His was a mixed calling. He spent two days a week pro bono at the clinic for the hospital ministering to the needs of the sick, and poor of the immigrant East Side. He was so beloved and respected, the Republican party renewed offers to run him on the Republican ticket as Congressman for the East Side. His true duties where elsewhere, in a packed clinic. Wherever he was, he cast a shadow, he was six and half feet tall, of elegant and patrician bearing, soft brown eyes, his voice of baritonal warmth, his huge hands were gentle. At Xmas time, he was seen in the charity wards distributing gifts and cookies baked by his wife, Emily. He lived in Gramercy Park, he would see his patients even within its snobbish insularity from the rest of the city.

Tony was unloading coal at a landmark brownstone in Gramercy Park, the home of Dr. Henry Nash. He was done. He saw a light in the library to the side of the building. Dr. Henry Nash was reading, seated in a wing backed chair. He was alone. Tony tapped on the window, Dr. Nash rose from his chair to reappear on the threshold. He led Tony to the seclusion of a porte cochere. Tony handed him

the letter from Laetitia Abercrombie with self conscious noncha-
lance. He had a premonition the doctor was waiting for him, and not
the letter from Laetitia. He never saw the doctor at home.

"Tony! I need to talk to you, it's about Teresa." He led Tony into
his examining room which was dimly lit. An X-ray screen was illu-
minated. Dr. Nash pulled up a chair for Tony, then he moved to the
screen and inserted a film which revealed the lobes of lungs. "Tony,
for sometime I have been worried about Teresa's chest. I have been
waiting for you, you deliver every Wednesday at this hour. I brought
the X-rays with me from the hospital to show you. At first I hoped
what I saw were only scars from bouts of pneumonia when she was
younger. The X-rays were not definitive. We did a biopsy and many
sputum tests, those shaded areas are tubercular lesions."

Tony rose, his legs shaky, he approached the screen. He saw dark
areas on the upper and lower lobes. Tony began to sob, rubbing the
screen as if to erase the lesion markings.

"Now, with proper care, there is every chance she will recover and
be well."

"Anything, anything! What must I do?"

"She needs immediate care and treatment. I shall have her admitted to the city hospital for tuberculars."

"On that island, the East River?"

"Yes, she will find adequate care."

"No! Not there, I heard stories!"

"You have no choices, Tony. A private sanitarium is beyond your
means."

"Where are they?"

"Upstate, Saranac, in the Adirondacks."

"We send her there."

"The cost is prohibitive."

"I will find more work."

"Teresa told me you are working yourselves out of debt and you were returning to school. She tells me you are captain of the math team at City College."

"Tessie comes first."

"If you insist, I'll make arrangements. If you don't mind, I'll pay the admitting fee and you can pay me back when you can."

"Thanks, I'll manage."

Tony dried his tears. He must put on a brave face when he sees Teresa. "I'll manage." That phrase was empty brag, that first crocus of April in a bronze planter mocked him!

He found Patsy in the front office on Kenmare Street surrounded by coffins of burnished woods and silvery metal, a few in bronze, one gold plated. It was noontime, Tony sat on one of the portable folding chairs used in viewing rooms. No viewing was in progress.

Patsy looked at the gloomy face of Tony.

"By the looks of you, you came to pick a coffin for yourself?"

"Patsy, I hate to bother you again. I got a problem."

"I hear you go back to school, give up wagon and route, and lottery. Big mouthful!"

"Tessie is sick. She must go to a sanitarium upstate. I got to make money to pay for it."

"No school, eh? Too bad, you smart young man."

"You must speak to Don Capodiferro about expanding my route so I can afford to see Tessie looked after."

"Old Ironhead?"

"Will you speak to him?"

"Listen *bene guaglione*, you know I bought a piece of the lottery bank from Don Capodiferro."

"That's why I bring you the lottery slips?"

"*Managgia*, you bring me no slips, you remember everything, *ambo, terno, quaterna, cinquina,* e tom*bala.*"

"It's easier, slips can be lost."

"But they stick in your head! *Meraviglia!* you make no mistakes. People kill you for a *terno*, if you make mix up!"

"About expanding my route, will you speak for me to Don Capodiferro, Patsy?"

"And why not, Tony? I look on you as a godson, I have no son. I wish you, my son, so you respect me. I tell Don Capodiferro you are my godson, must be good to you, too. Understand?"

"I am honored, Patsy."

"Now, I talk to you like a son who can be trusted to death. Don Capodiferro and the boys get ready for end of bootleg, lottery is peanuts. Talk about future, maybe you be part of future. So you stick around. Now, speakeasies and night clubs need plenty ice. I speak Old Ironhead he give you night clubs, speakeasies from Battery Park up to Harlem. But no Harlem, belong to Dutch Schultz. You wait, I phone him now."

Patsy went into his inner office to phone. Tony could see him gesticulating, placing his right hand over his heart, as if taking an oath. He hung up, and gave him a thumbs up.

"Thanks, Patsy, but how can I cover that route with a horse and wagon?"

"Patsy think for you already. You sell horse and wagon, I give you old hearse, no look like hearse after paint job. Big old fashion hearse, big enough for ten coffins, big for forty cakes of ice. Enough for day's run. You make enough money to pay for Tessie, later maybe you go back to school, and Tessie get better."

"Tessie comes first, Patsy."

"Now, Tony, always other guy. Maybe some guy push you around, you take over his route. We have muscle Tony, you have muscle. You no charge pennies for ice. Dollars, Tony, dollars, no *miseria!* You know how to drive, no? I teach you. You come tomorrow morning after you sell horse, and ice wagon. *Bene?*"

"*Bene.*"

Back at the stable, he saw a person at the far end sitting on a bale of hay. It was Don Capodiferro, gangster boss of the East Side. The meeting was planned by Patsy to get Don Capodiferro acquainted with the likes of him.

He called, "Antonio!"

Tony doffed his cap, and bowed slightly.

Don Capodiferro was thin, sickly, a face deeply creased, a pendulant nose, and thin lipped. When he spoke words were pressed and fluted.

"I understand from Pasquale you are man to be respected, your father was, your mother, we come over on same boat from Italy. Pasquale tell me of bad *mala fortuna* with sister, you fine brother. Antonio, we *paesani*. Me, and Pasquale help you today, tomorrow you help us, eh?"

"It is a point of honor, Don Capodiferro."

"Bravo, Antonio! Well spoken."

"I never forget a courtesy."

"I understand—*una cortesia, bene,* we shall see."

CHAPTER 9

1935

The heart of the Great Depression Tony was twenty four years of age. The years went by swiftly, almost mindlessly, as Tony slogged at work, never finishing the rounds before eight or nine in the evening. Teresa was still at the sanitarium. He spared no expense in guaranteeing the best medical care. His every Sunday was spent with her in the Adirondacks. Every Spring, as if deceived by the vernal hopes of the season, he was told Teresa would recover. The truth was Teresa needed ever more expensive and critical care. When he was too tired to sleep, he fingered the medallion given to him by the now Monsignor John Keenan. He read up on the saint Albert Magnus, or Albert the Great, one of the greatest intellects of the Middle Ages who averred that the book of nature is not written in the language of mathematics, and he rejected Pythagorean doctrines of the supremacy of numbers, that nature was a mathematical formulation. Fundamentally, it was a theological tease that medallion, and a challenge to possess statistical evidence of chance or necessity, he could perhaps argue a doctoral dissertation on the question. Mr. Horowitz, his math mentor at City College, still nagged Tony about returning to school when they met at Veniero's for coffee. Tony wore the medallion, a haircloth to remind him of the problem he set for himself. A sensuous equation?

Tony put school on the back burner until Teresa was declared cured one hundred percent. He now had exclusive route of the night clubs in lower New York and the Village, and uptown to the limits of Harlem. He no longer picked up lottery plays. He now owed a Reo truck, he junked the make shift hearse. He was on call all hours when the clubs ran out of ice. He served the Copacabana, the Embassy El Morocco Club, Jimmy's—Speakeasies gone with the bootlegging when Roosevelt repealed the Volstead Act. Tony grew a couple of inches, he now stood six feet two and his physical frame got heavier. He had an apartment on Sullivan Street in the Village. So many jazz clubs in the Village, he could hand cart the ice. Patsy Paglieri began to brag about his godson, how he held his own when guys tried to rough him up and take over the route. All by way of saying that Tony was well liked and respected, even if he was only twenty-four years old.

Frequently, Patsy came to him with a problem at the lottery bank about figures and odds. Tony poured over the records matching winners and losers and calculating odds and percentages. Patsy shared a Havana cigar with Tony to reward him and marvel at his dexterity with numbers and retentive memory. For a lark one evening, when Patsy brought him some dubious accounting, Tony to show off, repeated the plays of a previous review which left Patsy whistling through the cigar smoke. Don Capodiferro, who owned the lottery for lower New York, relied on him to adjust the odds in his favor. Tony often thought of his father's customers and penny world of ice and coal. He went to a recital given by Carl Sobieski at Town Hall. Whenever he was in the ghettoes of the Old-Law tenements, he dropped by to see the retarded twins to bring milk and clothing, to say hello to Birnbaum, Natale, Cleary, Van Brunts, De Fiore, Nussbaum, Minna, Vincenzo,—

Although, he was making enough money to support the high cost of the sanitarium, he missed the old customers. He treasured the blue book of his father, he often thumbed through it, nostalgically.

Time changed, fridges were common appliances. Most of club trade was shaved ice for the bars and blocked ice for chipping. Business was dwindling.

The age of the iceman was over. Every week one or more iceboxes were abandoned in hallways, and garbage dumps; or given to Tony to get rid of. Of all sizes, and many years of use, they stood mute witnesses to the changing times. Tony stacked them in the stable for sentimental reasons as if deserved to be retained like old servants. The ice boxes, in some cases, held their own as furniture: ice boxes as chests, in four compartments, some likely sideboards, many of solid oak and maples, paneled, carved designs, and ornamentation. Webber astutely catalogued the trade names; White Mountain, Maine, Siberia, Eddy, Leonard Cleanable, Belding-Hall. He reprinted an ad already quaint in the eyes of many by Frigidaire putting down the ice box. It sold for five dollars, already the ice box was on its way to becoming quaint.

Frigidaire's ads cited the inconvenience of ice as a refrigerant: Often the iceman does not arrive when we expect him. He sometimes tracks up the kitchen floor and causes annoyance. The delivery of ice in the ordinary way can never be looked upon as a very sanitary proceeding. The reason for all this has been the conditions, rather than the desires of the ice man and waiting for ice. This is a further annoyance that is often caused by the fact that some member of the household wants to leave, but cannot because the ice has not come.

Passing Derek Webber's second hand store on Bleeker Street, he saw chairs, tables, and antiquated gas and oil lamps for sale on the sidewalk. It occurred to him the cast-off ice boxes had some worth as curiousities of a fading past, or useful as chests, stowaway furnitiure. He explained this to Webber who agreed to take a look, and bought them all, about fifteen, instead of selling outright, he became a collector of ice boxes. Webber, was also a painter of some skill, he gave Tony a painting of Teresa copied from a photograph taken at Ulmer

Park. Teresa sitting on a prow-like storm-breaker stone looking out beyond the Narrows to the Atlantic Ocean. The frame was antique, oval, and ornate.

Every Sunday at visiting time, Teresa was a nag, harping on school, and blaming her ill health for frustrating his career. Last time she ordered him to bone up on Differential Calculus.

It was early June.

Teresa took him by the hand which was feverish to the touch. "Come, Tony, I wish to show you my haunt by a stream." She led him to a mountain stream bordered by giant rhododendrons in pinkish bloom and young lacy hemlocks. They were standing hand in hand on a rock ledge, looking down on falling water of a stream in Spring freshet, fuming a rainbow mist.

"I often come here, Tony. Did you know as the water splashes and bubbles it releases oxygen? I find it easier to breathe standing here. Do you feel it?"

"I do, sis. You should come here often."

"It is a long walk from my room. I mustn't linger, because of the puffs of pollen."

"You must not stay too close to the flowers, or too close to the end of the ledge, Sis."

"And if I did, Tony, and slipped off the ledge, wouldn't it be better here than dead in my room?"

"Now, Sis, that's foolish talk."

"I am here more than five years, Tony. I am missing a lung and half of another. Don't believe what the doctors say. I am dying, dear brother."

"And what shall we do with the pastry I brought you from Veniero's? All those butter cookies and macaroons. Let's go back and have some tea with the pastries. I feel a sneeze coming on," Tony said with forced jocularity.

"I'll gorge myself to make you happy."

Tony stopped by Patsy Paglieri. Patsy was having dinner in the apartment above the funeral home. The aroma of *ragu* sauce could awaken the dead in Patsy's coffins below if a viewing was in progress. Patsy invited him to a dinner of *bracciolatini* and meatballs stuffed with *pignoli*, and pork butts, and yes, there was a plateful of ziti left over. Tony thanked them and accepted a glass of wine. Mrs. Paglieri and the daughters, age twelve and thirteen, respectfully asked about Teresa.

"Not too well, signora Paglieri."

"That too bad, Antonio, *dio mio che castigo!*"

He peeled a large orange, segmented it into four fingers of wine. Mrs. Paglieri and daughters hurriedly cleared the dishes and discreetly removed themselves from the room to allow the men to talk.

"*Ebbene*, Tony?"

"Patsy, I need a loan. I am back in my payments to the sanitarium. It is strange Patsy, the less hope there is the more the cost."

"Wisely said, Tony." Patsy wiped his lips vigorously with a napkin.

"I don't want to go to the shylocks."

"You bet, I understand. I ask question, how come you no skim, you no play cards, no casinos, poker games are all over city—you clean up. Long as bosses make money, you make few dollars on the side. You tear up sale slips and keep money. You *genio*, you stupidly *onesto*, and now you go borrow money from shylock with vigorish 300 percent. I speak to Don Capodiferro, he loan you money no interest, he know you stupidly onesto and smile. He know you need money you break the boss's bank in New Orleans if you want, you *genio*."

"Patsy, I need another glass of wine, I had a bad day."

"Brutto, brutto ti compatisce."

"Patsy, you always have a place in your heart for me. Thank you. What I said would sound better in Italian, Patsy, but I know little Italian."

CHAPTER 10

When Tony got back to his place, a telegram was waiting from the sanitarium telling him Teresa was in critical condition. He got back to his Reo and headed for Saranac as fast as the Reo could go. When he burst into the front door of the sanitarium a heavy dread throttled him. Tessie was dead! It was noontime, the sun was blazing hot, but Tony was trembling, his speech was a staccato gasping. A reception nurse told him to wait while she paged the doctor on duty. He showed up rubbing his eyes. He had been napping after a long night.

"My sister, Teresa Di Napoli!" Tony grabbed his lapels. The young doctor said, "You got word, sir."

"She is better, right?"

The nurse at the desk mouthed his sister's name until the sleepy doctor fully understood the party referred to. "Mr. Di Napoli, release me please, so we may talk in the visitor's room."

Tony instead, gripped his arm. "Take me to my sister!"

"Your sister passed away an hour ago. I was up with her all night, nothing we could do, we are surprised, she was doing well, a massive hemorrhage, we could not stop the bleeding, we gave eight quarts of blood."

Tony crumpled, his knees gave, he could not straighten himself, the nurse left her desk to help the doctor to haul Tony to his feet.

They held on while he staggered to gain control of his legs. "I got to see her!"

"Not at this moment, you see, only two hours ago, certain preparations are necessary."

The nurse added, "The room must be tidied."

"I want to see her now, maybe she is still alive."

The doctor moved to the emergency bell for security, Tony saw the move and stopped him. The nurse retreated to her desk behind a handful of folders. "It is against all regulations, Mr. Di Napoli, you may not like what you see."

"Maybe, I can comfort her, a last word, a goodbye kiss."

"Mr. Di Napoli, you force me to be plain spoken, your sister is brain dead, nothing you, or I can do anything more."

"I want to see her now!"

"Will you sign a paper you forced me to violate regulations."

"Later! Take me now!"

Tony should have waited until the nurses had tidied the room, and the body. When he rushed into the room, he almost fell over his sister's body on a morgue gurney spotted by blood. Tessie's skin was wrinkled, yellow-white like old paper, her body was drained by the hemorrhage. Her head lay aside on the stained pillow, her mouth gaped which had not been strapped. Perhaps, her last move was to look at the photograph of Tony on the night table. The doctor was shaken by the unnatural sobbing that shook Tony jerkily like a mechanical toy. He shut the door and made no report.

Later, the nurse brought him a cup of coffee while he signed a release to turn the body over to a local undertaker who will transport the body to Paglieri's Funeral Home. The nurse kindly explained that a tubercular lesion can explode like, and flood the body with the bacilli, and—."

"It's okay, I'm sorry nurse, half my life is gone."

Tactfully, the nurse asked, "Will you grant permission for an autopsy, the staff is puzzled by the sudden eruption."

"No, no, let her be, let her be."

The viewing took place at Patsy Paglieri's funeral home. Many young people unknown to Tony brought flowers, laid them at the foot of the bier, and introduced themselves as fellow patients. She was interred in the same grave with her mother and father.

The pastor of St. Anne's, now Monsignor John Keenan, read a High Mass for Teresa. Although Teresa was absent more than three years, the church was half full. More than a few listed in Domenico's blue book attended and extended condolences to Tony. Instead of Mass cards, Tony suggested a donation to the American Tuberculosis Association. Tony bought a deed for grave for Teresa and himself in Fourth Calvary, and ordered a headstone with an chiseled epigraph he once saw in a dream:

HOPE LIES NOT HERE BUT WHERE JOY LIVES FOREVER

And.-Tony consoled himself with the frequent company of Monsignor Keenan in place of devotions or prayer. He was convinced he was temperamentally unsuited for prayer.

When persons first met Monsignor John Keenan, they had the impression of meeting a human monolith of muscle and bone. He played tackle for Villanova and a candidate for All-American. His head was square, made even more so by a pompadour. His nose was scarred and tilted to the right side of his ruddy face. He was a great hand-shaker and mixer. Parishioners avoided that handshake that numbed fingers for hours after. As a preacher, he was entertaining, always had a joke from the pulpit that madw sunny the candled gloom. He was a sportsman, avid for a game any time, touch football, squash, handball, tennis. Like many sportsman, he enjoyed side bets. When he won a side bet in a friendly match, he primed the money basket for the Sunday Masses. A lucky start, hoping for a full basket of bills, and little silver. As a seminarian, he cracked his books casually like a gamesman, yet he excelled in Canon Law.

Tony was his favorite opponent and handball buddy. Tony graduated to handball from stoop ball, and box ball, where the sidewalk flagstones set the court. Father bet friendly sums with Tony that he always won, the scores were always tight. As Monsignor of St. Anne's, Father Keenan began a drive for funds to build a playground for the school that involved the purchase of a condemned tenement and its demolition. The drive was well supported by Tony and others, but the rumor was that Monsignor Keenan had raised most of the funds from gambling. The playground was built, and the priest took care the asphalt was marked with boundary lines as a handball court, and a springy, wooden back wall installed. Most Saturday mornings, he and Tony played a match, or two, the priest stubbornly not allowing Tony to win one match. On summer afternoons, they stripped to the waist under a burning sun, the medallion gleaming.

As a Monsignor, John Keenan could be flippant in his off court talks with Tony as they showered and dressed in the Monsignor's residence.

"We play as opposite partners in a sport, actually we are apart in thought. I know you are busy in your flat, according to all the books in your place, you are a university onto yourself. Every book I pick up says something about theories of probability, your marginal equations are in every book, Tony you never left school."

"That's the way my mind works."

"You must know Tony, that the church, on and off, has proscribed theories of probability and chance. The goddess Fortuna was the most popular semi-deity of Rome, her statues were destroyed at the end of paganism. The church says God's will rules all actions on earth."

"Wouldn't it be interesting to discover who is right?"

"With an equation?"

"Father, let's face it, you enjoy gambling for small stakes, you play the Italian lottery for the hell of it, and you always have fifty bucks on Villanova. You challenge me with the medallion."

"That's true."

"Einstein said God does not throw dice, but he never proved he didn't. You are thrilled by an occasional gamble, I am thrilled by formulations, right or wrong about probability. In a word, John, it is exciting. I play in the court of probabilities. Father, you know I have no solid opinions on this open question, for or against."

"You are a skeptic, if not agnostic."

Patsy could not understand a grown man playing handball so frequently in a schoolyard until Tony told him he found it difficult to pray in church, or out, that he could not accept the merciful image of God, or his saints. If there was a God, he could not forgive the early death of Teresa. It was a bone in his throat if he uttered: I believe..."
Yet, he felt a need for consolation after the death of Teresa and his nearness to Monsignor Keenan, as friend and competitor assuaged part of his guilt for not praying for the soul of Teresa, his father, Domenick, and mother Rosa.

CHAPTER 11

Tony answered, unshaven for a week, eyes as red a stop lights.

"What are you doing? Sitting *shiva*?

"I know, I got to get back on the route."

"Forget the route, no more ice and coal for you, no more."

"I am going back to school. I promised Tessie."

"Don Capodiferro has plans for you, that's why I come."

"I squared a grievance. I want a new life."

"That's what Don Capodiferro say, a new life for you."

"Another club route to cover Brooklyn, too?"

"Why you don't read the papers? *Finito*! This new time!"

"Give my excuses to the Don."

"You want him to come here personally? He is the Don, you come when he says so. Shave, get dressed. I'll wait for you in my car."

Don Capodiferro was playing solitaire at Patsy's desk at the funeral home. He rose and walked solemnly to Tony and kissed him on both cheeks.

"*Mie condoglianze*, Tony."

"Thank you, Don Capodiferro, about my route—"

"No, no. I no have you come for route, you too *intelligente* for ice-man. You are a *genio* with numbers. You remember and figure good. Let's see, I show you thirty cards for half minute, I put cards back in deck, you tell me what cards I show, eh?"

"I don't do card tricks, Don Capodiferro."

"This no trick, you show me *genio*. Patsy count half minute," which Patsy did.

Don Capodiferro replaced the cards in the deck. "Now, you tell me what cards you see?"

Tony called off the cards correctly.

Don Capodiferro beamed. "Patsy, you bring pencil and paper, you write down 5378943421 times 56498765, you write down good, Patsy?"

"Got it."

"Now, Tony what is the so*mm*a?"

"He means the sum." said Patsy.

Tony wrote down the sum on the paper.

"*Mama mia!* Patsy, you see what I see?"

"But how we going to prove the *somma*."

"I tell you it is the correct answer. *Benissimo!* Tony, time change, no bootlegging new world, where we make more money, eh? Thank God we still have the Italian lottery, but something happen bigger than lottery called policy. We need a *genio* to run the operation, the bosses have *poco* smarts and need *genio paesano* to keep good accounts. We no trust Mr. Braunstein, sure his idea, he say clean out the suckers with nickel and dime plays. This bigger than moonshine, Tony, bigger small time Italian lottery, policy soon."

"With due respect, Don Capodiferro, I am planning to go back to school."

"What for? You know more than *professori*! And, then you make salary and grow old. Tony, you are *bello*, young, enjoy yourself. All school already in your head. You go to Phil Kronfield you tell Phil give you two suits, you see Joe Aiello of Packard, he give you new car, what else you want, eh?"

"I need to study mathematics, it is my passion, Don Capodiferro."

"Even I, an uneducated man, understand this *passione*. But you study the same, you buy books, at the policy office you live with *numeri*—."

"I am sorry, I promised Tessie."

There was an embarrassed pause. Don Capodiferro as a gentleman and a Don did not wish to mention the $6500 he gave outright to settle the bill at the sanitarium on Tessie's behalf.

"A promise is a promise, and we are men of honor. I say this, you try for three months, get policy game started, we no trust Braunstein then you go back to school and become *professore*, eh?"

Patsy out of the Don's sight was signaling, "Yes, yes—you owe him the balance for the sanitarium."

"Three months?"

"*Sicuro*," averred Don Capodiferro.

"Agreed three months, no longer?"

Don Capodiferro's arms drew Tony and Patsy to his sides where they stood as if photographed at a confirmation.

Back at his flat Tony needed a machete to get to his couch, books and papers were everywhere. Three years accumulation of self-study. On the couch Tony surveyed the landscape. Was he a bit too coy, wasn't he eager for the new job, playing field of chance and of probabilities.

It was often remarked by many the strangeness of Tony's disappearance from work, or handball, especially by Monsignor Keenan who joked Tony had gone on to a retreat, but he knew that Tony could be found in his flat working with tables and graphs, desperately. Monsignor Keenan surmised there was more to this seclusion that met the eye, in some fashion Tony was indulging his passion for mathematics. His friendship with the Monsignor was a comfort blanket that drew him away from that solitary oneness and oneness of numbers.

Tony cherished Teresa's one volume library, the sonnets of Christina Rossetti. Often he read it, paying attention to her markings on sonnets over which she enthused and rhapsodized. Tony tried to share her feelings for they were in synch on most matters. Of course, the poems were pretty with lovely turns of speech and phrases, only he could not share the same emotions in which Teresa participated. Instead, he found himself admiring the symmetrical perfection of the poem, the stresses, the metered line, the rhyme scheme, the couplets, and the formal limits of the fourteen line sonnet. He could not feel as intensely as Teresa probably felt, he saw the sonnet schematically, an arrangement of integers with no poetic resonance. As a matter of fact, doodling, he created an equation for a sonnet which remarkably gave him a sense of an elusive poem.

The Poem

Remember me when I am gone away,
Gone far away into the silent land;
When you can no more hold me by the hand,
Nor I half turn to go yet turning stay.
Remember me when no more day by day
You tell me of our future that we planned:

Only remember me; you understand
It will be late to counsel then or pray.
Yet if you should forget me for a while
And afterwards remember, do not grieve:
For if the darkness and corruption leave
A vestige of the thoughts that once I had,
Better by far you should forget and smile
Than that you should remember and be sad.

His mind began to figure an equation fro the sonnet. He backed off, Teresa would not approve.

An item in the World newspaper from a bundle of dated newspapers he once collected to fire the kindling in the stoves of the cold water flats. Casimir Kodaly, artist, was found dead in his flat. The cause of death was a dislodgement of a rubber hose leading to a Bunsen burner from a gas feed. The portraits? He stopped back on his rounds. The landlady said she burned them all in the coal-fired furnace, the last batch an hour ago Ragged smoke hovered over the building and fingered southward to mix with the smoke from the chimneys of the Edison Company. For an instant, Tony imagined, passing overhead, charcoal sketches of the sitters at the Municipal baths.

CHAPTER 12

In the morning Tony reported to the lottery headquarters located above the Blue Grotto Café on Grand Street, a dilapidated building, dusty and dirty, and plaster peeling from the walls. A long counter faced the door, and crossed the room. Along a side wall was a battery of five phones. On another wall an enlarged blackboard facsimile of a lottery slip in checkered squares. Whoever was there was expecting him, someone was quickly at a peephole in the door, satisfied, he opened the tin lined door. Tony saw a a one window room, mostly bare of furniture except for a planked billiard table and a scatter of wire chairs. On the walls were faded posters of Italian resorts supplied by shipping lines, Tuscany, the Amalfi Coast, Mt. Etna, Capri. An elderly man was at telegraph machine tapping. A middle aged man with a broad moustache sorted policy slips on the huge table which seemed like an impractical way to place them in order. The third man who greeted him silently directed him to a chair near the telegraph machine. He stared incredulously at Tony, "You're just a kid! Is this a joke?"

"If you have any questions call—."

"No, no—."

The operator at the telegraph machine stopped tapping, turned to get a better look of Tony. "Stefano, this is the whiz kid the Don told us about." The operator got up and shook Tony's hand, his tapping hand trembling from overuse. "I am a former telegraph operator on the SS Augustus. Arnaldo at the table worked for the tax department of the province of Campania years ago in Italy.

"Ignazio, can speak for himself."

The greeter bowed with a smile, "My name is Ignazio Porro, a former professor of mathematics at the University of Pavia, at your service."

"I was told to give a helping hand for three months, I am going back to school."

Ignazio, mathematician, took a swig at a bottle of grappa, wiped his mouth, placed his hand on Tony's shoulder. "At last a colleague! But so young a colleague, more like a collegian."

"Thank you, I am in luck, you can tutor me."

"Tony, we know your name, the Don has raved about your prowess. I can teach you higher mathematics, those who are gifted with numbers are born, not taught. Of course, you understand that mathematics is not nimble calculation or remembering numbers, as you demonstrated with the Don. He brought me your quick sum of the multiplying test he gave you. And, you were correct to the last decibel. Why should I be friendly to you, you are taking my job, yes, I know, that's the way it is—"

"I assure you sir, only a trial of three months."

"Tony, I make a bargain with you, I am not a young man anymore, I drink too much, I live alone with my books, they say after twenty-five, a mathematician has done what he will ever do in the field. You have time ahead of you. I am a derelict on the path to a grand theorem. Until recently, I was also an adjunct professor at Fordham, the Jesuits don't like a tipsy professor in classrooms. So I am here, *Eccomi!* So tolerate me young man, I need the job, let me stay on. I'll help you in every way."

"If its within my power, I say stay, and I look forward to working together."

"My job is to set the odds every day, Arnaldo sorts the lottery slip winners and losers, and Stefano at the telegraph gets the tax reports from certain provinces in Italy on which the lottery is based. You will be heading a brand new operation called policy based on pari-mutuel numbers from the racetracks, it is the brain child of Braunstein, and Mike Miranda, the grand *consigliere*. I will remain with the Italian lottery, I was told, as you launch the policy game in the city. The Jewish and the Italian brains claim it will reap millions. Soon, like an aged number counter, I will retire, go back to my rooms to study the mystery and fatality of numbers, not so innocent, Excuse me, I did not offer you a drink. I have an unopened bottle in my locker."

"I thank you, not today. I must familiarize myself."

Ignazio pointed to a desk with iron supports in a far corner. "I piled the latest racing sheets on the desk, so you could familiarize yourself with the pari-mutuel betting. In due course, I understand, the betting could be based on any series of numbers, even those on cereal boxes. Perhaps they can get the children to break piggy banks and play, too."

"I have never been to a racetrack. I am interested in theories of chance and probability."

"Would you say that luck runs in circles, and why?

"Pi is so close to circles. Everything in the universe is the fruit of chance. Or the most important questions of life are problems of probability."

"We will go downstairs to the café across the street and we chat. Soon the runners will be crowding the counter with lottery slips, and vile *Toscanis*. On these chits of paper, the players drape their dreams, losers in the end. It is your task as in lottery or policy to see no one wins consistently against the bank, lose, yes. These lottery slips are incarnated hunches, wishes, desires, dreams, hopes, regrets, freedom from the day to day boredom, tedium, an ennui that insinuates, permeates, and makes us desperate for anything new, not the same sameness, until the mockery of death, death holding your losing ticket in his hand. A grave with such a monument is apt for me. I'll get my hat, we go to the café and have a long talk. Your youth somehow impels me to talk at length, and I am afraid, foolishly. Come. We shall discuss Cardano and talk about the rarefied rambles of others perplexed by the gambler's toss, heads or tails." He stopped before a huge yellow poster of the Italian tombola, the lottery dream book roughly illustrating dreams in numbered boxes.

Ignazio laughed mockingly. "Make a wish Mr. Di Napoli. Or throw a dart at any box, the chance of the day. Ah!"

One of the club stops of the closed out route was located on Sullivan Street, only two buildings from his flat, it was called Jimmy's, the most popular night club in New York. When he delivered ice he had to pass through a narrow hallway that abutted on the dressing room of the six chorines who were the show girls of the floor show. As he passed, the door was left open to get rid of perfume gone acrid and odors of body sweat in the stuffiness of dressing rooms. Chorines often teased him by baring a long leg, a breast that slipped out of a brassiere, a plump backside, calling out to him begging his attention. When he looked away, they laughed at his shyness, he was a mark for ribaldry.

During a match Monsignor asked Tony if he would take him to a night club. He was on the Mayor's Committee who had moral misgivings about burlesque and night clubs. He had seen burlesque, thought it harmless, crude farce diversion to keep the unemployed thinking about the Depression. Would Tony take him around to a club so he could gain an appreciation of any moral significance. Tony agreed. Without his collar agreed. Without his collar Tony introduced him to Jimmy's. The Monsignor appeared to enjoy himself, he saw no harm anywhere, he thought it was a classy joint. The Monsignor was a booster for anything that broke through the dark clouds of the Depression, a new dance, a ballad, a new cocktail. He, asked Tommy Lyman, the male soloist to sing a few of his favorites. He was a sport, and a good tipper, everyone liked him not because he was a Monsignor, for he was recognized. He was a regular guy.

Among the showgirls at Jimmy Kelly's, Tony was sparked by the newcomer, younger than the others, sprite and saucy, she did not bait him, but stared at him provocatively. He decided to revisit. No older than eighteen or nineteen, as tall as Tony, who could qualify for Ziegfield follies, she was turned down because she was a half inch too tall for the posing and tableaux. Her hair was flaxen, with a touch of gold in sunlight, a milk white complexion and marble blue eyes. With a mite of makeup, she was still a natural beauty. He asked for a date, she gave him an unenthused yes. He met her after the last show at two a.m. outside the club. Her name was Clarise.

"Walk me home, Tony. I feel like talking. The girls talk only about men, last dates, and dirty jokes—"

"Sure, sure, where to?"

"On Charles Street."

"That's a short walk."

"We will walk slow."

They walked on silently.

"Well, say something Tony."

"It's a beautiful morning in New York."

"Well, what shall we talk about."

"It's up to you for openers."

"Okay, why are you an iceman?"

"I was an iceman."

"The girls say you are some kind of a wizard with numbers."

"I am handy with math."

"Do you know at the last club I worked in Cincinnati, there was an act where a man told fortunes by the numbers in your life, birthdays, license plate, address—he was very good. Can you do that?"

"It is called numerology. I don't practice it."

"Shame, with your gift. The girls explained you are an iceman to support your sister at a TB sanitarium."

"You been checking up on me."

"It's talky-talk anyone one of them would have you, if you had money. They are looking for sugar daddies and drunken millionaires."

"And you?"

"The same," she said saucily.

"And, you are here with poor me."

"You ever been in a mining town in Montana? The riches are below ground, above are the piss poor—but desolating, Tony, desolating. When I left town, I swore I would be rich one day, on top! To be rich, Tony! How old are you?"

"Twenty-four."

"Next Wednesday I shall be nineteen."

"We'll celebrate."

"Why not? I gave myself two years to marry a rich man, when I am your age I shall be rich as can be! Then, you can be my lover."

"Wow! You are something Clarise! So cold-hearted."

"Didn't I say you could be my lover? What is one thing got to do with the other. I want to see the gold they dig out of Montana by the sweat of my father miner back on my fingers. Is that asking too much?"

Tony laughed at her impudence. "You are a gold-digger!"

She clapped her hands in approval. "Yes, yes that's what I am a gold-digger." She leaned her head on his shoulder. "And you will be my lover. I will cuddle you in my furs."

"Well, not exactly a gold-digger, Tony. Am I beautiful?"

"You are nifty."

"Then I deserve beautiful things, a fair trade, isn't it?"

"You sound like a procuress."

"What's that?"

"A woman who sells women, only in this case, you are selling yourself."

"A self-procuress?"

"You got it."

"Well, then that's what I am!"

"You must have been born with a brain forty years old."

"Speaking of being born, this man I was telling you about in the night club show told fortune by numbers. I mentioned this to you?"

"You did."

"Well, backstage, I asked him for mine. He asked for my birth certificate, I mean my birth date which is April13,1913. Instead of reading palms, he reads license plates, laundry tickets like a magician read palms."

"What did he foretell?"

"Only this, I would die in Montana. He was wrong, that's the last place I want to go back to dead or alive. Did you ever tell fortunes with numbers?"

"To tell you the truth, if I tried numerology, I'd feel like sinning. That's what my sister said."

"With no disrespect to your sister, it is a silly remark."

"You see, Clarise, God is supposed to guide our lives not chance."

"So every time you play the lottery you are sinning? I must tell the girls they are going straight to hell, they play every day. I take my chances on a rich husband. All the Ziegfeld girls marry millionaires. I missed the chorus by a half inch. There, you see Tony, numbers again!"

"Try the Vanities."

"Too tall again, all the girls are dancers, and don't pose girls my height, can't dance like the short ones."

"A lot of millionaires patronize Jimmy's."

"I know, I know, that's why I work for 30 bucks a week. There is one who has been eyeing me three nights straight, I don't know his name. You ought to see his diamond tie pin and rings! And what will he get in exchange for those rings, a virgin, that's me."

"You are putting me off the first night out together."

"No, I am being honest, for his money he gets a first edition, no second editions. We are both young. Tony, no sex. I am saving myself, its my investment. Maybe I'll get to love him."

"Sex is a pawn then?"

"Night and day that's all the girls jabber about. It's disgusting. What they do for a dinner at a swanky place is unimaginable. It is shocking."

"Clarise, I can't keep my hands off you, so what am I doing here side by side under a full moon?"

She squeezed his arm. "How romantic! You are young, and loony, and beautiful, and probably a hot lover. What I want is a man like a cold jewel."

"I am not a cold jewel just a hot iceman! I can't wait to kiss you goodnight."

"That's permitted but no hanky panky."

"Speaking of jewels you are the fire in a star sapphire."

"Tony, you are so poetic. You can try to seduce me, it will be fun, won't gain you anything below my garter belt, there I gab like the girls! I know you are a gentleman Tony, and will keep your place."

"Keep my place? You do sound old-fashioned."

She laughed. "Don't you know, Tony, I am an old fashioned girl! I must marry first with a big diamond and a gold band. If I kissed you once, I would be done for, and riding your ice truck for the rest of my life."

"I am going back to school as soon as my sister Tessie is better."

"What for?"

"I am not sure, maybe a mathematician."

"Wow! Do they make much money? Never mind. I'll be proud of you and you will also be the hot lover of a rich lady with a Park Avenue address."

"Clarise, your brashness frightens me!"

They met the next morning after the last floor show at Jimmy's. A line-up of limousines were parked outside the awning of the walkway. Clarise pointed to a Pierce Arrow trimmed gold and black like one of Patsy's deluxe hearses.

"That beauty belongs to Arnold Braunstein, he sent me flowers, and promised an interview with Ziegfield to reconsider my turndown. He is going to make arrangements for me to meet him privately. What do you think of that?"

"Right up your alley."

"You don't mind?"

"Why should I? There's nothing between us."

"I am fond of you, you know that."

"Do I?"

"Don't I tell what's in my heart?"

"Heart? That's a steel trap."

"You are plain jealous."

"You gave me no reason to be jealous."

"He told me, Florenz, that's what he calls him, is going to cast for a new show at the Winter Garden, it's all posing and gorgeous gowns."

"He is not bulling you, he knows all the show people of New York."

"Is he a booking agent?"

"Arnold Braunstein is the biggest gambler in the country. And he bankrolls Broadway shows."

"Why do I always get stuck with number guys, the girls tell me you used to pick up lottery slips, that's gambling."

"Watch your step."

"The girls say full steam ahead, he can make me a star, he is single, and lives at the Plaza in a suite."

"Don't think he is going to be your patsy, that's a high-powered guy with friends in the worst places. And, he runs booze from Canada to Boston Jimmy gets his booze from him. He is an international bootlegger."

"Should that make a difference?"

"How do you mean?"

"I have an appointment at the Winter Garden tomorrow afternoon. Should I go?"

"Let's see, you want to rope a millionaire, and that he is, and he can make you a star. How can you nix that?"

"I like it."

"Go to the audition then, and see what happens."

"The girls tell, they know everybody, and you are aces, you are good to your sister."

"Right now I don't feel good."

"That's because you are jealous right?"

"You are too chancy!"

"That's what lottery numbers are all about, no?" "I left Butte with a train ticket and fifty-five dollars. I tell you what, you wait for me on the stoop and I'll tell you what happened. As you say in New York, I got a break. I got to keep my mind on business. Tony, I am beginning to like you too much and you might sidetrack me, so I must do what I planned all along from Butte to New York."

"Casting people have couches at auditions, be careful, don't sit on one, or you may be lying on it, your legs the air."

"Tony, you are silly jealous."

CHAPTER 13

Tony was at the stoop around six in the evening. He looked up at her window, it was dark. Nine o'clock and her window is still dark. He flagged a cab directing him to the Winter Garden. It was dark there, too except for the stage door exit light. He knocked. The watchman said there had been no rehearsal and no audition that day. Back to the apartment, and still no light. It was five in the morning when a Pierce Arrow pulls up from which a woman is pushed out of the slow moving vehicle. He saw a rumpled dress, flaxen hair, and legs awry in the gutter. Clarise! She looked like a mussed rag doll He picked her up, she was limp, she moaned with pain and whimpered…The sun rose to reveal a face caked with blood, her nose appeared flattened, her forehead was swollen, her hair stuck to bruised cheeks, a bloody foam oozed out of her mouth. His stomach rose, he was about to retch. He swallowed hard. No handbag, no key, he must kick open her door. He gathered her together as if she were disjointed and carried her to the third story flat where he kicked in the door. He placed her on a divan. He was undecided whether to call the ambulance first, or tend to Clarise. She needed emergency care! In the bathroom, he filled a basin with warm water, grabbed a towel, and returned to her. Her eyes were blackened and half closed. She pushed him away. "Don't hit me anymore, I'll do anything you say!" Tony forced her prone, and began to wash her face, her nose was swollen and not broken, he untangled clotted hair. No panties. He noticed blood trickling between her legs. He washed her there too, but the blood trickled still. He saw her vulva enlarged and inflamed. My God! What did he do to her? She recognized him with a wan smile that became a grimace of more pain when she tried to open her caked lips to speak. She kissed his hand. "I must get you an ambulance."

"No, no Tony stay with me, don't leave me."

She sat up, she felt her nose. "Is it broken?"

"Bruised, my God! What happened?"

Her voice was a cackle through split lips. "He did it, he did it!"

"I'll call the police."

"No, no. Tony, you'll get hurt too. Help me to the shower, I clean myself up and you take me to the hospital."

Tony carried her into the bathroom, stripped her of the muddied and blooded dress, and placed her in a warm bath. He soaped her clean. He placed a robe around her, led her to the small bedroom and placed her in bed.

"I am so ashamed Tony. I should have died."

"Do you have any brandy?"

"There's a cordial in the pantry."

He got the cordial and she drank it in sips.

"Tell me what happened."

"I went to Winter Garden, there was no audition."

"You should have turned back."

"He said Mr. Ziegfield would be at his apartment, when I got there we were alone. Then, he said he would make me a star but I had to join him in quirky sex. I was leaving, he grabbed me, dragged me to the bedroom, and did terrible things to me, terrible! I resisted, he beat me like a madman, and then—" she covered her face with a pillow. He heard her muffled voice say, "He stuck things into me, not sex, but things, and covered my mouth to stop my screaming."

The bedclothes were blooding. She was hemorrhaging. "You got to go to the hospital now Clarise. You are hemorrhaging!" Clarise grew faint now from loss of blood. He picked her up as she was naked under her robe hustled down the three flights and hailed a cab for the nearest hospital emergency. She was admitted at St. Vincent's Hospital. He waited two hours until she was out of danger. When he was told she was resting the admitting doctor was accompanied by a policeman with a note pad.

"From our preliminary examination there is suspicion this was a botched abortion, we are not sure at the moment. The officer needs your name and identifying information. You must know that abortion is a crime."

"Are you guys crazy? She was raped with instruments!"

"Now, who's crazy," said the officer with poised a pencil. Tony was out the door, and running. Where? To the hotel, to see Arnold Braunstein.

He hopped a starting taxi, opened the door wide to the astonishment of the cabbie, slipped in and directed him to the Hotel Plaza. By the gilt clock in the lobby it was ten o'clock. He asked the clerk at the front desk for Mr. Braunstein's suite. At the door, a maid emerged carrying a heap of bloodied sheets. Tony eyed them savagely which frightened her. "Man, he have bloody nose," and she rushed past him leaving the door ajar. Maybe his Sulka shorts was among the laundry! Ah! He entered a large living room studded with vases brimming with tall gladioli. He heard the gushing of water, his eyes located the bathroom down a short corridor. Braunstein was showering behind a translucent door. Braustein saw his dark shape behind the glass.

"Is that you Chang? Give me my silk robe." He thought Tony was his valet.

Tony pulled the shower door off its hinges, grabbed Braunstein by the throat and hurled him against a tiled wall. Tony dragged the stunned gambler into the living room.

"Just you, and me. Mr. Braunstein. Call it an audition."

"What audition?" he gasped.

"Clarise, remember Clarise?"

"You mean that cunt."

Tony lifted the body of the portly Braunstein and slammed him against the mantel of a fireplace. Braunstein's face turned blue by the loss of air in his compressed lungs. Tony raised him to full height, and uppercut his balls and groin. Braunstein's face writhed in agony, his eyelids fluttered like a fast moving fan. Tony's fist hit on the jaw and he heard it crack. Braunstein's face was lopsided and grinning grotesquely. The timed TV came on with a calm voice announcing local news. It brought Tony to his senses. "No! you must not kill him," said the announcer, or so Tony imagined. He released Braunstein who fell in a heap on the carpet holding his groin. Tony heard a key in the door, as it opened, he bowled over the valet. He took the staff elevator express to the ground floor. In fifteen minutes, he was back at St. Vincent's. The admitting doctor apologized about his suspicions. Clarise would be discharged in the morning, she was now sedated, and resting. He could pick her up tomorrow. When he got there at ten in the morning, he was told she signed out and left a note.

'Dear Tony, I am going back to Butte. I guess the numbers were right on the money, I am going to die in Butte an old lady. I have a regret that I never kissed you. Clarise.'

CHAPTER 14

That evening Patsy Paglieri was waiting for him as he parked his truck in the garage. Patsy's face was long as a cortege on the way to Calvary He wagged a finger disapprovingly. "You bad boy, Tony. Deep, deep trouble?"

"A club run out of ice."

"No fool with me Tony. Let me see fists."

"Why?"

"Let me see fists, okay?"

"Scraped them shaving ice." He bared his bruised fists.

"So it's true."

"What are you talking about?"

"You in big trouble, big guai. You pick on wrong person."

"I'll be straight with you Patsy. The guy is a monster, he deserved whatever he got! You won't believe what he did to that girl."

"From Jimmy's—the ash blonde—what's her name"

"Clarise."

"And you almost kill Arnold Braunstein because of her?"

"She was a nice kid."

"Did you ever lay her."

"No. Like I told you, she was fresh from Montana."

"And you are the fresh kid from the East Side. Where is she now?"

"Went back home."

"Good, that's one out of the way, now about you."

"How do they know it was me?"

"Cabbies are gabby, pass the word around, it comes around."

"What happens now?"

"Well, today, tomorrow, a car will block your truck, two guys come out, grab you, push you in car, the car heads for Arnold Braunsteins cabin in Sullivan County he still owns has a dozen stills run by moonshiners. Arnold will wait for you. You be beaten up until pretty face caves, then Braustein will tear off balls, and prick, and stuff them in mouth. You die a cocksucker."

"I got to get out of town."

"Where you go, will be waiting, Braunstein owns wire service from coast to coast. You are *effutato*."

"What does that mean?"

"You are dead."

"I was born yesterday."

"It's your ass now in sling."

"Why, why do you come to tell me I am dead? To get paid beforehand for my funeral?"

"You surprise me, Tony. Much surprise. I walk away, and you are finished."

"Patsy, you say there is a way out."

"Yes, yes, but listen to your friend Patsy, who save your life."

"I am listening Patsy, for me and Tessie."

"Can you forget her for a minute?" Patsy took Tony by the chin and held it firmly. "Look in my eyes show you I came help you for your father's sake, and *beata* Tessie too—and you, you good but *stupido*! boy! Don't interrupt when I talk. You ready?"

Tony nodded yes, Patsy still gripping his chin, now released it.

"You almost kill the biggest man in rackets in the city, the Italians on Bayard Street in his back pocket. His pays off cops, politicians, the governor, feeds the pigeons that shit on City Hall. He is big brain, no carry a piece, no strong arm, never arrested, a gentleman gambler.

He does not bruise his knuckles on nobodies—he is a killer in his heart. I know what you tell me what he do with this girl, happen before, other girls too go to hospital. He no can get it up so that's the way he gets his kicks."

"I tell you what he did—"

Patsy put his fingers to his lips. "We know. When I hear you in trouble I go and see Don Capodiferro to save you. He wipe his hands. You die the way Braunstein wants you to die. None of his business. But I say, girl make fool of you. He laughs. He stop laugh, he think, he say you his *paesan*, and what to do! He say Braunstein expects schooner to unload two rumrunners at twelve mile limit off Gravesend Bay, seventy-five thousand dollars of genuine Scotch, last time three of his men killed in hijack. Don Capodiferro is wise, he say Tony has truck, get another one, Tony does the pickup of Scotch, what he got to lose if Tony get killed better than vendetta of Braunstein, balls and prick in the mouth, capisce. So I say whose is other driver. He say you Patsy, you stand up for him, but he make trouble between me and Mr. Braunstein. Me! Me! Tony, see what you got me into? The Don blames me for what you did! I never rode protection for any bootleg!...I say yes. He call up Braunstein who won't listen, he wants you with your balls in your mouth. Don Capodiferro raise his voice and Braunstein say alright he suspected the Don did the last hijacking. It was a guarantee of shipment, and would keep Tony around for the pickings later. Don Capodiferro say he take five cases of Scotch for himself, all for friendship sake." Tony threw his arms around Patsy and kissed him on both cheeks.

"I hope its not the kisses of death for you and me."

"Patsy, I owe you my life!"

Patsy shook him off. "Why, why people say you so smart? You big jackass with broads! That cockteaser!"

"But, Patsy I thought bootlegging was over."

"Braunstein got warehouse in Canada full of Scotch. He got word of raid. He must move to the States. We be on the last bootleg.

Braunstein gone legit with the booze with Johnny Walker all the Scotches and rye. He smart, he saw future."

"Patsy, I owe you my life!"

Patsy shook him off, "Why—why people say you so smart? You big jackass with broads!"

That evening two trucks met at St. Mark's Square, Tony's Reo and Patsy's leased Ford, the Ford led the way along Ocean Parkway to Coney Island. Once out of the city on Fourth Avenue in Brooklyn, Patsy hailed Tony to stop and handed him a revolver.

"I don't know how to use it."

"Just pull the trigger hard if some guy aims to kill you. In Calabria I killed a man who killed my father, who killed his father—*una vendetta*, never end—so I take boat to America. Watch my back, and I watch you, okay."

Satisfied that no hijacker was trailing them, the lead Ford turned into Mermaid Avenue, made a sharp turn into a side street that ended at the Coney Island Creek, and parked above a slope that fell to a shore of seashells, and driftwood. The Creek was at high tide running strong from Gravesend Bay. The night was moonless, you could hear the tide mounting in the narrow waterway. Tony, and Patsy slid down the slope, and waited for a signal from the incoming rumrunners. On the incoming tide, the almost retird, high speed Liberty powered rumrunners could cut their engines and glide silently into the Creek One big willow overhead on the bank of the Creek kept swathing them with limber branches There was an off-shore breeze. After an hour's wait, they heard the dip and wash of the prows of the rumrunners. The first boat flashed a lantern, and Patsy answered with his torch, a firefly's glow. The sky lightened as a gibbous moon rose over Staten Island. Both boats were low in the water loaded with a cargo of burlapped cases of Scotch. The hulls scraped gravel beds. A sturdy plank was placed across the distance from boat to shore in reach of Tony and Patsy. Two men manned each boat, garbed longshoreman, with baling hooks across their chests. Patsy crossed the plank, gave them the agreed password, and the two crews began to load the trucks with cases of Canadian Scotch, uncut. Patsy and Tony stood guard. In two hours the trucks were loaded, the springs groaned. The boats turned about in the narrow Creek motors purring until they sprinted all out on reaching the open Bay, then gunned again to reach the safety of the schooner waiting for them twelve miles out to sea. Patsy led again, with Tony close behind on an unlit causeway. A half block away a car with four men swerved in front of them, blocking the trucks. Patsy and Tony saw the gleam of revolvers pointed at them, and downward, ordering them to descend from the cabins, and surrender the cargoes. Patsy began shooting, not with a revolver but with a double-barreled shotgun that strafed the four men standing before them with two bursts. They screamed as lead struck them in a swath. Patsy sprayed the car, the windhield exploded to splinters of glass which slashed the hijack-ers. Tony's revolver was frozen in his fingers. One of the hijackers crawled under the limited trajectory of the shotgun and stood on the running board with his gun at Tony's head. Tony's elbow caught him in the throat, he gasped and fell beside the truck as if gaffed. Patsy signaled to Tony to move while he kept the hijackers at bay with spo-radic bursts from the shotgun. From nowhere a hijacker was astride the hood of the Reo. Tony fired, the revolver jumping in his hand, he aimed for a shoulder, and he hit his mark, the hijacker grabbed at his shoulder, and rolled down to the cobbled street. The two trucks now accelerated into a well lighted Cropsey Avenue and lumbered north to the Manhattan. Tony was in a clammy sweat, he felt an exhilara-tion he was ashamed of. Patsy waved a well done, and the trucks cruised safely to a warehouse on Remington Street.

Braunstein was there backed by three goons.

He ordered Tony off the truck. Tony said, "We are even."

"Your ass," said Blaustein, "you going answer to me privately." He turned to his men, "Put him in my car, I'll juggle his balls on the way to the cabin."

It was not to be. Don Capodiferro strolled into the warehouse. "Something wrong, Mr. Braunstein?"

Braunstein glared, then backed down, and called his men away back to his blue Marmon.

Patsy set aside five cases of Scotch for the Don.

CHAPTER 15

1935

President Franklin Roosevelt was president, relief rolls are rising, a percentage of dole money was played on the lottery and on the increasingly popular policy game. Controllers of the game racked up enormous profits that served only themselves. A big win, a *tombola* in the lottery, or a 1000 to 1 shot policy win revived the spirits of the East Side, and they played more recklessly. Fiorello La Guardia was demolishing slot machines, and organizing committees to monitor burlesque theatres, and lewd performances. Tony glittered in the eyes of the East Siders, they knew who he was, and what he did, he was the golden boy in charge of their destinies, he set the odds and the rules of the games. The local charities, synagogues and churches, despite La Guardia's thundering played on the side for a good cause, an orphanage, school desks, a playground, a new steeple, a new boiler. And, Tony glittered in a mirage of gold, now twenty-five years of age he was strikingly handsome, fancies custom tailoring, Sulka ties, Italian *borsolinos*, and the best straw Panama hats in summer. He was no showboat, always a natural reserve about him that commanded respect, and an alert intelligence in his eyes that told by-passers that this was no ordinary *boulvardier*. And, however, resplendent in expensive togs he had the common touch which made him well-liked by all.

Actually a regimen for Tony he had to tear himself away from his interminable studies at night and early morning on a project know to himself alone and Professor Sol Horowitz at City College. Monsignor John Keenan who visited his flat one day unannounced found a morass of charts and tables, and piles of paper slips blocking his way. The debate between chance and divine will. When he strolled down Second Avenue, people turned out to look at Tony, some superstitiously wished to touch him to bring them good luck. Like a God, Tony was above the law. As in Tammany days, the cops and Fusion politicians were paid for a hands-off arrangement. If he lived long enough, Tony would become a legend, a flamboyant dresser, a mathematical wizard, and a generous heart, for years he supported a tubercular sister at the best sanitarium in the country slaving on an ice truck. Tuberculosis made them all cousins. He was a mensch, un glantuomo.

It was commonly known he was absentminded, lost in thought, forgetful, his canes and umbrellas and hats were left unclaimed at the stores on Second Avenue.

He was told by the Don to go to Harlem to give them a blueprint designed by him for Harlem policy. He got to the Cotton Club about a quarter of nine that evening. There was valet parking so his Packard Phaeton was in trusted hands. As he entered the club, he was flanked by white couples in swanky dress. He had the notion the club was for black patrons only. Blacks were not permitted as patrons. The club had a black staff and black entertainers. He never wandered this far uptown, it was not home ground. A tall, black man person appeared to be waiting for him at a floor table as he was watched the door. When Tony checked his hat, the black man directed a waiter to bring him to his table. Dudley Jones was the black subaltern to Dutch Schultz who owned the joint. Dudley was impressive given his height and beautiful tuxeded suit that modeled a muscled body. On a massive head he wore glasses the size of pince-nez which was an affectation. He seemed to apologize for them catching Tony's curiosity.

"These," he laid them aside, "I bought on my trip to Paris. Ever been to Paris?"

"Never, I don't mind them."

"Hey! We must be able to look each other in the eye in this business."

"Half our business is already over. Mr. Jones, only some details in this envelope. He laid the envelope on the table. "It's the whole policy package drawn by me."

"Mr. Miranda says you got a Jewish brain in the body of an Italian, that's what he says, and that's good enough for me, yessir." He laughed with his diaphragm. Duke Wellington's band struck up the opening number. Dudley Jones pushed his chair back for a better view to hint they could resume after the show. A mulatto chorus line trooped on to the oval dance floor dancing to the Duke' jazzy arrangements. The staff was darker skinned, and the patrons were uniformly from table to table, white. The girls beautiful in hues of light darkness, and danced with a great sense of rhythm. Dudley beamed on Tony to say isn't the show terrific? When the chorus finished off with a can-can number, the spotlight picked up the soloist singer of the evening. To Tony's surprise, she was ebony black with the gloss of high polish, the features were so very fine, fine, as in a faceted diamond. She was lithe and moved with an aristocratic grace. Her voice was not sultry, or what was characterized as coon shouting, but light, and penetrating in perfect pitch. Her creamy white gown was spangled with gold designs. She reminded Tony of an Ethiopian princess one saw in the newspapers covering the war then in progress between Italy and Ethiopia.

"Who is she?"

"Yvette Dickens, you like her?"

"She is a standout."

Dudley laughed. "Because she is black?"

"No, she has talent."

Could there be something vaguely familiar about the singer? He moved his chair closer to the parquet dance floor. She saw his move, and stared at him curiously, now singing to him with gay animation. Dudley pulled his nose. "Mr. Tony don't get any ideas, she is not allowed to mix with white patrons."

After the singer finished her number, and bowed, she did not step backstage, but stepped forward to walk in Tony's direction. He stood up to greet her. She placed her hands across his face as if modeling it, then exclaimed "Tony Di Napoli! Tony Di Napoli!" Dutch Schultz was frowning behind the stage curtain, and motioning to call her back. It was against the house rules to fraternize with white patrons. And on the dance floor! She embraced him impulsively, while he stood stock-still. She sat him down beside her. "Don't you remember me, Edna, Tessie's girl friend."

Tony embraced her, tears in his eyes. She wiped them away with part of the halter to her gown. "Edna Severance!"

"Yes, yes, Edna. I, you and Tessie, we played in the hayloft of the stable. You gave me my first ride on the back of a horse, Jim was his name!" Tony smiling broadly could only repeat: "Edna! Edna!"

"How's Tessie?"

"She passed away."

"O! I am so sorry! Both of you were my first playmates. The only children who would play with me."

Edna lived with her grandfather a shack behind the stable. Her grandfather's name was Egbert, he spoke with a faint cockney accent picked up from English jockeys while acting as a handler of race horses at the Sheepshead Bay track. He groomed the finest horses in the stable of Edward the Seventh when he came over for the Brooklyn meets. When she about thirteen, Edna moved somewhere, unexpectedly.

"What happened Edna, we asked and looked for you?"

"When Egbert, Grandpa died, I was alone. The Children's Society placed me in a home and sent me back to school. So here I am, with you my childhood crush!"

Tony blushed.

"Didn't Tessie ever tell you I was in love with you."

"I—I."

"I fantasized I was going to marry when we grew up, Tony. You were as good as hitched, then one day I woke up with a shock that it could never be."

"Times have changed Edna."

Edna laughed lightly. "Now, Tony, seriously, are holding out any hope to a very black girl."

"Edna we were all fond of each other."

"I see you Tony, and my little girl's heart goes thump, thump, can you believe it? Even now! Tony, I got to ready for the next number. See me after the club closes, I'll met you out front. We must talk more of the old days." She kissed him on the cheek. "Don't stand me up!"

Dudley said: "Would be good idea if you stood her up, she's Fred Johnson's girl."

"Who is Fred Johnson?"

"He is my boss."

"Nothing wrong, we are old friends, that's all."

"He's in Detroit for a few days. When he comes back, take a powder. Now, let's get down to business." Tony reviewed he contents of the package on the table which was the plan for the operation of the policy racket. Dudley excused himself to deliver the package to Dutch Schultz who was fuming and frowning over the antics of Edna and Tony in front of a full house. Got to draw the color line!

Tony waited out front until the club emptied of staff, and patrons, and still no Edna. His Packard was running at the curb. He glanced at his watch that read 3:30 AM. Why did Edna put him on, that she was so eager to talk of old times, and renew an old acquaintance?

From a side door, he saw three men emerge, one of them was Dutch Shultz, who lowered the brim of his hat, and walked briskly between two bodyguards to a Buick Roadmaster down the street in which they roared off almost deliberately swiping his Packard.

Tony got into his Packard, and drove home to St. Mark's Square. When he got off the elevator at the top floor, he saw someone hunched against his door. It was Edna!

"For goodness sake, what kept you?"

"You told me to wait out front."

"I know Tony, I know, they were watching me."

"Dudley, and Mr. Schultz."

Tony opened his door and both entered the apartment. He switched on the lights revealing a living room scattered with books, the scent of his Russian cigarettes still in the air. "This my hayloft now."

"Looks like you are doing your homework," she said as she reclined on a couch. "You use to help me with arithmetic, you were a good teacher."

"How about a drink."

"At this hour, I am ready for bed, do you mind."

"Mind what?"

"That I stay until morning."

He sat beside her, and held her hand. "I have to touch you to believe Edna Severance is beside me."

"Better than the shack, eh Tony, and the stable? People from the tenement threw down trash from the airway alleys that landed on the roof of the shack like heavy rain day and night. Grandpa, and I got used to it, like you and Tessie got used to the L train rumbling past your flat. We slept through all that, didn't we? And now we are together again, no trash hitting the roof and no L trains."

"Edna, no idea what this night—"

"Morning."

"Means to me. You see all these books lying about, they are all puzzles I try to solve, math puzzles, I think I am going to discover a theorem of life's ups and downs. But you here tonight by my side, that is a greater puzzle."

"Tony, dear, I am beat, have you an extra pair of pajamas for me. Where shall I sleep, on the couch."

"My bed, I'll take the couch. I'll place the pajamas on the bed."

"I was always trusted you."

"Edna, you are like a sister to me."

"Don't say that Tony, it is not what I want to hear. I'll explain in the morning, kiss me goodnight." He led her to his bedroom, prepared the pajamas and kissed her goodnight on the forehead.

She smiled and singsonged, "Tony, Tony, are you blind?"

"What did you say?"

"I said if anyone comes to the door, do not open it, okay."

"Goodnight."

"Goodnight."

It was about ten when Edna walked into the kitchen wearing his silk Sulka pajamas, and robe. Tony had breakfast going since eight o'clock. She sat down ate the French toast and part of a day old muffin, and three cups of coffee. The coffee was a bracer to give her courage to say what she had on her mind.

Tony took no initiative for the day, he waited for her to finish. He was just plain happy to see Edna across the table, that once stringy black girl playing hide and seek in the hayloft was this beautifully exotic woman. He never noticed her eyes were a light blue, her teeth were evenly white, her brow was high, her hair was coiffured Egyptian style—Ethiopian, Egyptian. He must have been gawking.

"Didn't you ever serve breakfast to a negress?"

"Edna, don't use that word, please."

"That's what I am Tony, that's the divide between you and me. When I realized that when I was thirteen and in love with you, you did not know did you, I confessed to Tessie, you know what she said, she said tell him you love him. We were children! And—yet Tony I wanted to die, I hoped a trash bag from a high window would strike me dead. How romantic, Tony!" She laughed, then her blue eyes flickered. Last night you said you thought of me as a sister. I always thought of you as my lover whatever that meant to a thirteen year old. The sight of you last night filled me with that little girl's longing. You excite me as woman. Tony will you stop looking at me as if I was Tessie, and love me for who I am Edna Severance." She bowed her head as if she had committed a sin.

"First money I made Tony, I brought a gold earring to mask the cleft on your ear. I still have it, you can screw it on. My little toe on the my left foot was partly nibbled away. So I took up singing. I can't put a earring on my small toe, can I?" They both laughed. Edna fastened the erring on Tony's ear, and kissed it lucky.

"Edna don't offer yourself to me, I want you, too. I did not sleep a wink, twice I came to your door wondering if I could—"

"I heard you, and tiptoed to the door hoping you would open it, we are acting like two adolescents. What a wonderful feeling!"

He embraced her across the table. "Now that we are once more together Edna, we must not part."

"We'll make love dearest, Tony all day if you wish then I must get back to the club. You must not come to see me again. Mr. Dutch Schultz doesn't like the idea of café au lait."

"What do you mean?"

"When you make coffee with cream, you mix black and white. Tony, what do you do, what were you doing at the club, it looked like business."

"Difficult to describe what I do, let's say I am the odds maker for the policy game in New York."

"Dudley told me you are a walking brain, but I see muscle, too. And me, Tony, did café au lait ever satisfy the creamer? Imagine, I auditioned for Langston Hughe's play Mulatto, he says what are you doing here? You are black! This from a colored gentleman. Come, make love to me. Come, Tony I can't wait, hold me in your arms."

She closed her eyes, and her limbs trembled.

When Edna left for the club around seven in the evening, she warned him not to see her at the club again. She would come to him at his place. When she saw Tony at a front table that evening, frightened, she missed a repeat of her blues ballad. He sent persistent flowers with a card, 'Forever.' On the third night Dutch Schultz strolled to his table, and offered him a drink. Tony refused. Dutch Schultz looked back at Edna on stage.

"Don Capodiferro tells me you are smart and I believe him when I looked at your operation's manual for policy in Harlem. For a kid, you are awfully smart. In the case of the singer, why don't you smarten up?"

"We go way back."

"So I hear."

"So leave us alone."

"You did a great job, ready to roll. You are a stranger here. You don't know the rules, or the territory. The rule is you keep away from Yvette Dickens. Right now, you both been shacking up for the last three days at your place. Her boy friend is one of my enforcers, and he is a tough noodle. I got him in a cage in a rathskeller in the Bronx, two guys holding him down from going after you. What must I do? You are the Don's fair hair boy. I can't let you get hurt. You are too important to both of us, we can't read a gas meter straight. And, if you get hit by Fred Johnson, it means a war, and I don't want your Wops or Jews on my turf. Fred just took out a canary in Detroit, a favor to me, and my favor to him, is to get you forget Yvette. Do I make sense?"

"Not to me."

Dutch Shultz uncrossed his legs and stood up, leaned over and spat out: "Nigger lover."

Tony shrugged, Edna understood what was going on at the table, and fled to the wings. No need to skulk around anymore. He had it out with Mr. Schultz. All out in the open, Edna and him. Tony stayed until closing and waited out front hoping to drive Edna back to his place. Someone clapped a hand on his shoulder, he balled his fists. It was Patsy.

In Tony's Packard, Patsy gave it to him straight. "Don Capodiferro was told Dutch is unhappy about you. No one wants trouble. Broads are trouble. That black lady is screwing that brain of yours, you not screwing her. Dutch say pick anybody you like on the chorus line but she belongs to Fred Johnson."

"For the sake of our friendship, Patsy, don't say another bad word about her."

"You want to die over a dame?"

"I can handle myself."

"You couldn't squash a cockroach! The night of the hijack, you were aiming for the guys toes like you were chiropodist trimming toe nails. You got to listen to the Don, who likes you. You and dames! You are something, Tony! You love her, we like you, so—we got to choose, she goes."

He grabbed Patsy. "You wouldn't dare hurt her."

"No, no, Tony, but you ain't the only guy who got savvy brains."

"Suppose, together we leave town, hide out, somewhere?"

"Hide out, a black lady and a white guy on the lam, not a chance in a million. And, you know what Braunstein said to Dutch? He say "Waste the bastard, and stick his prick in his mouth."

"Where do want to be dropped off?"

"I am staying with you like glue, so you make no dopey moves. Those are my orders from the Don. Look, the LaSalle in the rear mir-ror has two guys backing me up. The Don says tie him up while we get rid of his black lady, black like *espresso*."

"You can't keep us apart!"

"Maybe you lovesick boy with no hair between his legs? Tomorrow, by this time I will play a *terno* with sixty-seven, it means you live a long life."

"You know the odds are fixed."

"You fix, that's what you do all the time. Now I fix, you don't leave my eyes until I hear from the Don, *capisce*? And keep your hand off the door handle, you make them guys in the La Salle nervous. We go to your place."

The sun rose, Patsy, and Tony were still up, staring at each other as if in a waiting room.

Patsy after making a phone call said he was told to wait on news. A half hour later the phone rang. Patsy, answered:

"Its for you."

A cablegram from Edna.

'Dearest Tony, When you receive this cablegram I shall be at sea on a steamer bound for France. Josephine Baker wired me offering me a role in her new review at the Follies Bergere. We must follow our stars. Goodbye, Edna'

CHAPTER 16

No one saw Tony for a week. With the loss of Edna it was like reliving the loss of Tessie. Whenever he was in the dumps, he hied over to the new playground at St. Anne's to play furious handball to work of his frustration or the blues. He was disappointed that Monsignor John Keenan was not around to give a match for he was a formidable opponent, and good for an exhausting workout to dispel cares of the day. Tony always took along three sweatshirts to cover his bare torso in relays during the matches with Monsignor Keenan. He played against himself until his palms bled like the hands of the crucified Christ in the apse of St. Anne's. Tony was told by the sacristan that the Monsignor was out of town.

Sister Clothilde watched the matches from her window in the adjacent convent between Monsignor Keenan and Tony Di Napoli. She approached Tony on the court because she believed they were close friends.

"Mr. Di Napoli, I am Sister Clothilde."

"Good day, Sister, I remember you consoling Teresa. I congratulate you on the new playground."

"I understand from Monsignor Keenan you are partly responsible, directly, and indirectly."

"That's an exaggeration, Sister, it is you two who have brought these improvements forward so the Monsignor tells me. You make a fine team."

"You think so."

"*Non pareil.*"

"How kind of you, Mr. Di Napoli, most kind. And you are a balanced team. You beat him on the count of the Sunday collection, and he beats you at handball, even-steven."

"With all due respect Sister Clothilde, prayer is passive for me. I work off sorrow, frustration by beating this black pellet against that stupid wall."

"Each in his own fashion, it is said." "Incidentally, we sisters had an imaginary bet on the Sunday collection plate, and you beat us as well as the Monsignor."

"I have a touch Sister Clothilde."

"Monsignor Keenan told us you are math whiz."

"Sometimes I wish numbers would leave me in peace, Sister."

"If I said pace would it help?"

"I need pace to an exponential charge to do me any good."

There was a pause.

"I should not be out here speaking to you Mr. Di Napoli, it is not seemly. My sisterly sisters are at the windows, don't look now, take my word. I am here to tell you that the Monsignor is in a bit of trouble. It appears there are funds missing from the treasury, large sums that the bishop has questioned, while the bishop is waiting for a response, the Monsignor decides to take a vacation. The bishop asks where has he gone. No one knows, he told no one of his destination, not a word to me but an indefinite note. He may be in trouble Mr. DiNapoli. I have heard that the Archdiocese is a bit incensed. Monsignor Keenan has great regard for you. Would you speak to him when he returns, he may need your help."

"Everyone deserves a vacation, Sister Clothilde, if we had to wait for a go ahead, we would never get off the ground. You can depend on me. Here's my card."

The Blue Grotto was almost empty this afternoon when Tony took a break from the lottery figures to order an *espresso*. Always present, on emergency call were two brawny men dressed alike in long capacious coats, and Homburgs. They lounged, bored, spoke to no one, at all hours, close to the wall phone, when it rang, they were the first to answer with alacrity, and dashed off into a Chevrolet roadster standing at the curb. Coat tails swung heavily as by a pendulum. Tony learned later the pockets were weighed by blackjacks, and brass knuckles. The two men were enforcers for shylocks, the finger breakers, the sluggers, and hit men for hire for the day. This afternoon, a phone call amused them, and they became talkative.

"Going to be fun."

"A crazy at Union Square preaching to the icemen."

"And Joe Meany lent him his ice wagon for a platform!"

Maurice, the poet, and Joe Meany were going to be slugged at Union Square. Tony was out the door, and hailed a cab. At Union Square, he spied the parked ice wagon, Joe Meany mutely by, holding the bridle of his skittish horse among a closing audience. Maurice was distributing his inflammatory poem, and ready to ascend the wagon for speechifying. Tony got to Joe Meany first.

"Joe get out of here fast, two guys are coming to beat you up."

"And, who's to say Anthony, that we are not within our rights?"

"Another time Joe, not now!"

"If it takes a revolution, Anthony, so be it. Read the poem by Maurice."

"Icemen! circle your wagons!
Defy all graft and payoffs,
Strike your chains, seize tongs, iron
Shavers, organize all scofflaws,

Of ice age laws and prisons!
Icemen! Circle your wagons!"

Maurice ascended the wagon. A brisk wind spread open his coat, his hair flowed with the breeze, his profile was slanted, he looked like a ruffled rooster.

Tony asked Joe Meany for a match, pretending to light up, as Meany dug in his pocket, he released the bridle. Tony slapped his horse on both haunches, the wagon forced itself through the crowd, into the open square, Maurice grappling helplessly with the reins. When the enforcers arrived they found a Square empty of Maurice, Joe Meany, and his wagon. Maurice and the remaining icemen were obsolete.

CHAPTER 17

To the East Side and the Village Tony glittered with gold when he walked down Second Avenue, or loitered along at Bleeker Street. In the years of his management, never were there so many winners, still more profits from the game than any place on earth. Tony appeared to be the Golden Calf, ironically in a time of the Great Depression. In the policy room a wall-sized facsimile of a blank lottery card was placed prominently, consisting of empty squares that would fill at the end of the day when the tax receipts of the principal provinces of Italy were posted after telegraph transmission from Italy. Listed were Rome, Naples, Bari, Florence, Venice, Torino, etc. A player chose a number along any line on the whole card, if you played *ambo*, you played two numbers, *terno* three numbers, *quaterno* four numbers. You played a succession of numbers across a line or all from a selection of ninety numerals. If you played all cities with a combination your card was marked X. On the right corner of the slip was the monogram of the policy outfit. On Fridays the numbers were amassed, recorded for all to see in Italian American newspapers, in this instance the Progresso. Slips were made out in duplicate by the runner, one for the player, one for the house. Runners collected all the bets, and piled them on Tony's desk. He made the calculation, sorted the winners without the aid of an adding machine discarded by Tony. The plays were in his head until he recorded them privately on several oak tag sheets in the flat marked with formulations. Very often he recognized his father's customers warmly, all still roosting in the old tenements.

Evenings, he holed himself in his flat and studied the lives of great gamesters of the past, Casanova who designed the first lottery for the King of France, and others. He pored over the astrological dream books, the ancient *tombola*, cabalistic numerology. Always the tormenting question, how to eliminate chance, and predict probability with certainty ever since humans tossed dice bones across the bare earth of Africa. Ever since man has been hoisted by the cycling caprice of the Wheel of Fortune, or unsteadily standing on the precarious globe of the ancient Goddess of Fortune. When he reflected in a quiet moment, he realized it was not such a bad life after all despite the imagined stigmata on his handball callouses. Often slips would pass his desk when he would recognize his customers of the East Side tenements which gave him a warm recognition. The Great Depression deepened in 1935, and half the East Side was on relief. Ragtime, and still the lottery and policy were more profitable than ever. Desperation increased the play. Yet, there were many winners that benefited in these dark days, the poor, churches, synagogues, the Newspaper Boy's Home, Henry Street Settlement House, etcetera. A lottery or policy win was like a glimmer of a firefly in a darkness of spirit. Tony looked at himself in the mirror. Did he see charity in his eyes? His secret? Get a grip on yourself Tony, you are not a bad guy really even if you are the brains of a racket.

Walking past the Thalia Theatre he saw an announcement on the billboard of a performance of the Dybuk adapted by Morris Grodin and starring Rachel Cohen. He bought a ticket for the matinee about to begin in twenty minutes. The Dybuk was familiar to him when he read about in reference to the role numbers played in the Kabbalah, about the twenty-two letters of the Hebrew language and ten numbers of the Septirot that would unveil the secrets of life. Although he knew no Yiddish, he was inquisitive about this ancient learning as it was deployed in the famous play. He had a seat center in the first row just below the stage. He was recognized by some in the early audience who smiled and wondered what he as doing at Yiddish all-spoken play. The curtain opened on a scene of a gloomy wooden synagogue somewhere in a shetl in Eastern Europe, occupied by rabbis, students and cantors praying. Tony got the gist midway in the first scene when Leah, played by the Jewish diva Rachel Cohen who cannot marry because she is possessed by a demon, a dybuk who is an ent whose life was unfulfilled on earth, so he returns to enter another body to live out a disappointed previous life. The dybuk refuses to leave the body of Leah, an entire scene is needed to exorcise the dybuk from the body of the beautiful Leah. There is a wedding and feasting. He was disappointed there was only a passing mention of the dangers of following the path of the Kabbalah which may lead to madness. When the curtain rose to much applause Madame Cohen took the last bow acknowledging a stamping ovation. Tony had expected a very histrionic acting, grand gestures, and long fainting spells, on the contrary she was as modern as Broadway, where in Tony's opinion, she belonged. What was admirable about her acting was its boldness, an independence of that quasi-oriental submissiveness of immigrant women. Her gorgeous red hair was flaunted, her large oval eyes were unashamedly intelligent among the elders of the synagogue. It is no wonder that the dybuk chose her for one more chance at life. He would have a glorious ride! Her face, and Tony was not being disrespectful, was that of rapturous Mary Magdelenes, also a redhead, in Italian paintings so sensuous and spiritual. He clapped so hard, Rachel Cohen took notice, and threw him a nosegay thrown on the stage. In an about face the audience began to applaud Tony for being so appreciative of their prima-donna.

A tall, stooped man in his forties motioned him to a side aisle.

"I am Morris Grodin the adapter of the bill you have just seen, may I have privilege of introducing you to my wife, Rachel Cohen? She asked to meet you."

"My pleasure, Mr. Grodin."

Tony followed the playwright to steps that led backstage. The actress was waiting for them smiling still in costume of that possessed daughter of Odessa.

Tony kissed her extended hand. As a a boulevardier of Second Avenue that afternoon, why not be gallant. Backstage, there was an aura of painless illusion of a somber play. No hurry to go back to the shambles of his apartment. Everything here denoted order, flats in place, furniture blocked neatly until a new play takes the boards, the predictability of a theatrical playbook, and mise en scene calmed his mind—unaccountably.

"I enjoyed your performance Madame Grodin."

"Why, Mr. Di Napoli you don't understand a word of Yiddish, you are a fibber."

"I assure you, one need no words, your acting was so eloquent."

"O! Mr. Di Napoli, you are really buttering us, I forgot lines and forgot an entire dramatic speech which my husband slaved over to make me a French Rachel." She laid a hand on her husband's arm. "He deserves a better leading lady."

"My wife, Mr. Di Napoli has trouble remembering her lines. She gets by because her audience is in great part newly arrived immigrants. Won't do for Broadway, and the national theatre circuit. She has already been scouted by Mr. Belasco and Reinhardt for a performance of Magda in English. But her memory is so unreliable, and yours I have been told is phenomenal. You see, Ignazio, a colleague of yours, played pinochle with my nephew who teaches math at CCNY. He spoke of you and said if you were playing pinochle, or bridge no one would ever have chance at winning, you were capable of recalling all the cards dealt, and not played. Have you ever played cards."

"No, it would be unfair."

"You say that with commendable fairness. Ignazio said you were a person of fine integrity although—"

"I am the plaything of policy."

"Morris, how could you?"

"Mr. Di Napoli, please accept my apology, I meant no offense, as a matter of fact, I admire you."

The actress sat down becomingly on a divan and listened attentively.

"As I see it we both seek certainty in our own way. For me Mr. Di Napoli, life is chaos. I make no sense of it. A well made play comforts me, although such plays are not well thought of today. Anything fortuitous, governed by sheer chance has no place here, all must be contrived to create neat universe before the footlights. I see my angst in your face."

"I live in an orbit of chance, as you say. Am I chance, do I govern chance, I don't know, sometimes I think I do, but that is monomaniacal madness."

"Morris get to the point! You are becoming a bore. Perhaps, you are only justifying your dramatic limitations."

"Now Rachel, that's not kind of you."

"I shall speak for myself. Mr. Di Napoli, I need to improve my memory, or I shall fail the big roles, imagine me doing Shaw, Ibsen, or Suderman floundering in the midst of the grandest language. You must have a method, a rote to help your memory, we are willing to reward you, although I expect you will not accept any gratuities."

Tony bowed. "Only the gratuity of your esteem and, friendship. Perhaps it was the dybuk who tripped your lines."

Mr. Grodin clapped, so did his wife, slapping her fan against the palm of her left hand. "Now let's see two weeks from now auditions will begin at the Belasco theatre for Magda. Do you think my wife will be ready?"

"I am at your service today."

"Wednesday, after the matinee Morris, we need a copy of the play-book."

"Would that be convenient, Mr. Di Napoli?"

"Suits me fine."

"Two copies, Morris."

CHAPTER 18

After the matinee on Wednesday, Tony sauntered by the stage carpenters setting up for the evening performance. At another end, painters were priming new flats for a future premiere. When he reached Madame Cohen's dressing room the door was open, she was waiting for him clothed in furs, her hair was tucked under a rakish toque of Parisian creation. Tony wore a light grey suit, a fawn topcoat, a wide silk Sulka tie with diamond tiepin, and a jaunty fedora. She slipped her arm under his and led him out to Second Avenue.

"Mr. Di Napoli, impossible back stage with all that hammering, we won't hear each other at all. It's a beautiful afternoon we shall sit on a bench at Stuyveasant Park. Besides, this new parfum from Paris is suffocating me, it will dissipate in fresh air. A perfume is like wine, it must breathe before use."

"Not too strong," he sniffed.

"Well, indoors scents are exaggerated, save us from cheap paint the painters are using on new scenery."

Water trucks washed Second Avenue that morning, the cobbles glistened like waves, the upper air shimmered in a golden haze. As they strolled arm in arm along the Avenue, all eyes feasted on the fashionable couple. Shop girls rushed to windows and doors to see what Madame Rachel Cohen was wearing, and they faked swooning at the sight of Tony.

Two beautiful people on the stage of Second Avenue, the Yiddish boulevard of dreams. They caused a ripple of applause passing by the Café Royale in the direction of Fourteenth Street. Tony stopped before the parterre entrance to Moskowitz and Lupowitz, the Rumanian-Jewish restaurant.

"Did you have luncheon, Madame Cohen?"

"Frankly, I am famished. I never dine before a performance."

He helped her step down to a lower level that led to the entrance of the restaurant, one of his favorites among the legendary restaurants of the East Side. Besides, he used to deliver ice and coal to its fabulous kitchen, and his father before him. So he was known to Mr. Lupowitz. Word passed around, Tony, the former iceman, was in the dining room, imagine with the diva Rachel Cohen! Cooks and scullions dodged the swinging door for a peek at Tony and his glamorous companion, Madame Rachel Cohen. Mr. Lupowitz came forward to greet them lowering his eyes discreetly. Discretion was a staple at the restaurant especially as to what happened in its private dining rooms.

He bowed with old world aplomb, his hand swept them towards a private dining room at an upper level. "What is your pleasure. Mr. Di Napoli, madame, I kiss your hand, you were superb in the Dybuk."

"Arthur give us a table where we can talk, and chill your best Tokay, and a light luncheon. I leave it to you," said Tony with a new debonair flair.

"I expect the evening crowd to drift in shortly. May I suggest a private dining room?" Tony glanced at the actress for her approval. She nodded with an airy wave of her hand. Mr. Arthur Lupowitz led them to the privacy of the deluxe establishment. The room was furnished with a table for two, a crimson couch in one corner, an elaborate standing candelabra with real candles, a heavily carpeted floor, and scarlet drapes that covered rear windows that looked out on a rear yard. The table was set with gleaming glasses, a laced tablecloth topped by a fluted vase with fresh flowers.

The actress clapped her hands delightfully. "Mr. Lupowitz, this is a stage setting for Tosca. Am I performing this afternoon?" He shied from replying directly. "Madame, you have the talent to be whatever you wish to be, you are the second Rachel to bring glory to the stage."

"You saw her Mr. Lupowitz?"

"Yes, at the Comedie Francaise."

"Mr. Lupowitz," she said slipping off her furs, "you are as charming as your establishment." Her afternoon frock was brocaded that fit the elegance of the room.

As he slipped a chair under her, he murmured, "May I suggest a roasted squab topped by a cherry wine sauce, an aperitif of Cheapeake oysters marinated with a soupcon of lemony rosolio, and—"

Tony deferred to the actress. "That would be delightful!"

Arthur Lupowitz closed the door behind him, and dispersed the kitchen help who were eavesdropping and snickering.

The Tokay was vintage 1909 and superb. Madame Cohen sipped at her glass refilled three times. Tony warned her with a smile. "Tokay is sweet but it is not candy wine."

"I love it! I never drank the expensive kind. And what you are saying is that if I have too much candy wine, I will flub my lines again. I shall be fortunate if I can move! I have partaken too much, Mr. Di Napoli and you only nibbled, I confess I was famished. To get into some of the costumes, to avoid those awful corsets, I set myself to dieting. I am reckless today." The two waiters unobtrusive as phantoms, only came by when the wine was low. One lit the candles of the cupid adorned candelabra which cast a soft boudoir light.

"I thought Mr. Cohen would have joined us."

She dabbed her lips carmined by the wine. "I am afraid he is not the best company, and he knows it, may I call you Tony?"

"Sure, and you are Rachel."

"Isn't that better, I think so. As I was saying, Morris is older than I, still his habits are those of a recluse. You would think that a highly gifted writer for the theatre would be a bit extravagant in his manner of living. A bit of panache. Not so with my husband. He lives to write, that is as concise an explanation I can offer. He was up this morning at three o'clock agonizing over a second act which as you know, is always the most difficult act in a drama."'

"He writes for you."

"He writes to satisfy that demon within him and this imp is determined to make his life unhappy, and mine, too. I am sorry. Is this confession time? We came here to rehearse, didn't we?"

"Isn't that the nature of the theatre, the real, the unreal, the joy, the grief, the intermediate ups and downs, the shaping of dreams?"

"In my husband's case yes, if his moods swung evenly. In a word, Tony, he is a depressive. If he were here now, he would be scribbling on this fine table cloth ruining it, utterly oblivious of you, and me. At those times, I don't exist at all, and when he is aware of me, I am a personage."

"I say write a comedy for me! He writes a tearful melodrama. Bring some gaiety to my life even if it is make believe." She winced. "There, there, I am beginning to feel sorry for myself. I am acting my personal chagrin!"

"He is an artist."

"Two artists living together? It is like two fledglings in a nest, one wishes to push the other out of the shared nest, to stand alone."

"You exaggerate, Rachel."

"Of course, I do, you are such a good listener."

"We had our coffee and brandy, shouldn't we go over some dialogue?"

"I warn you, I am lazy, my head is a mindless bubble of Tokay."

"I have been thinking of your problem. Do you sing?"

"I did some operettas."

"As you probably know from your husband, and his chats with my late assistant, Ignazio, as a man of numbers, I am conscious of timing, of meter, all speech on the stage is actually a kind of sing song of the words, so the use of portamento which is the bel canto art of moving from one phrase to another will carry you effortlessly on to the next phrase, the next cue, creating a seamless flow. May I ask you to sing a song."

"Here?"

"If you will."

Rachel begin to sing a light soprano, she sang the czarda from the Fledermaus. The waiters opened the door to hear better. When she finished the restaurant burst into applause.

"Rachel, you knew every word of the song. Did you ever forget the lyrics when you sang?"

"Never!"

"So why don't you emote in the same way, speak your lines as if you were singing, as if it were dramatic verse."

Her eyes brightened, "I believe you may be on to something."

"Did you bring a playbook with you?"

"In my purse, but dear me," she looked at her pinned watch, "we have been here three hours. I must get back for the evening performance. We'll met here again tomorrow, and we'll run through my part."

Perhaps, it was the décor of Lupowitz and Moskowitz that put Rachel off stride. She was spiffy a la Belle Epoque, a sequined frock, a lovely green chapeau perched derby-like, while her copper red hair flowed over her shoulders, and a silk scarf fell to her knees and a musky perfume. Tony reserved the private room with same table settings. Her eyes were heavy with mascara, a blush of rouge on her cheeks. This afternoon, Rachel was highly theatrical. Arthur Lupowitz made one error, flowers in the vase were long stemmed roses. The muskiness of her perfume and fragrance of the roses were joined intoxicants.

She said, laughing with gaiety, "Food will taste like attar of roses."

"The host suggested fresh striped bass poached with a golden mayonnaise, to begin with, a clear clam broth, Little Necks Rockefeller and a rare bottle of yellow wine from Moldavia from his private cellar."

"I shall miss that splendid bouquet of the Tokay."

Tony asked, "Do you have the playbook? We rehearse first or you won't care whether Magda lives or dies."

"Pages, too bulky," she slipped from her handbag four sheets of script and handed it to him. "Last night Morris rehearsed me. Keeping in mind what you said about *portamento*, the carry over. I did quite well. Of course, I stumbled. This morning I declaimed these four pages of script with only one lapse. I believe you have cured me, doctor."

"Words are more human than numbers, they have relationships. Numbers are haughty and independent, and eternal, not subject to heat, cold, a deluge, or the apocalypse, mocking you with one enigma after another, and they jeer boasting they will be around when we are gone."

"Please Tony, no heavy lifting this afternoon, I had my fill last night. Morris was restless, writing, gazing at a crescent moon, and sighing, believe me no one sighs as often as my husband, alas. No one sighs as deeply as a Jew. For Morris, that was no romantic moon, it was the scythe of death. To be with you Tony, is a reprieve from the company of a professional mourner. I tell him not to read the newspapers. He revels in self-pity. He is a Jewish Hamlet!"

"Rachel, did you taste the wine."

"Not yet. Is it fine?"

"A glory! Where is Moldavia?"

"Near Romania, I suppose." She sipped the wine. "I say it should be nearer!"

"I'll order another bottle."

"Please, please do, Tony, I am not sure if it is the wine, or you that gives me a lively mood. I haven't felt like this since the first time I fell in love."

"Who was he?"

"Can't you guess, a penniless actor with no talent! Consult my numbers, Tony. I was born—oops, I shan't tell, then you will know I am older than you."

"I don't tell fortunes."

"In the eyes of the East Side you are fortune itself."

"In the eyes of Morris, it's a cause for sorrow."

"You see how my husband effects people. What he does to me night and day, he is doing to you making you glum."

He poured the second bottle of the Moldavian wine.

"This will improve matters."

"It will make us forget Morris this afternoon."

"Do you wish to?"

"Yes, all afternoon." Her voice was husky. "There is no performance this evening. Morris has an interview in New York with Paramount Pictures, they need a screenwriter to guide Moses crossing the Red Sea. A spectacular, I understand. Morris will drown them all!"

"If Morris is away, we can catch the matinee performance of Cole Porter's Anything Goes. Or George White's Scandals."

She wiped the wine stain from her lips clumsily, and let fall the laced napkin. "You see that couch there in the corner? Take me there and whisper to me: You are a whore of Babylon, then make love to me. I shall not swoon. My eyes will remain wide open, Anthony, looking up at your gap-toothed beautiful face. You are magnificent, Tony. I will tie this scarf around your loins to pull you close, and closer to me. Come, or I will fake a swoon, and you will have to undress me! Come! I am swooning! Help me to undress!"

CHAPTER 19

Three days later Tony was at Phil Kronfeld's getting fitted for a tuxedo, Rachel was being honored by the Actor's Guild for the Best Ethnic Actress of Emigrant Theatre. She was shopping at Bonwit Tellers for a suitable gown. Tony was standing on a podium pestered by tailors when he became aware of this plain dressed woman at the window, who did not move. She could not be a window shopper, this was a haberdashery.

Measuring done, he stepped into the dressing room to get into his clothes. Phil would send on the Tuxedo customized from stock to his apartment in time for the ceremony at the Waldorf. He would pick up Rachel at six. He forgot about the woman at the window, as he stepped out of the store, she was beside him. He heard his name.

"Mr. Di Napoli, it is I, Sister Clothilde."

"I didn't recognize you."

"How could you, I am out of dress. I did not want to attract attention as a Sister in a strange neighborhood."

"Must be something important to bring you to this part of town."

"It's about Monsignor Keenan."

"When I did not hear from you I hoped his problems were over."

"He arrived this morning in a fearful state. I did not recognize him. He wasn't wearing his collar."

"He'll get another." Tony misunderstood the situation.

"He has locked himself in the baptistery. He won't come out. He was followed, he keeps saying, they will kill him! I said I will call the police. He replied,' No! Mother of God, don't tell anyone who asks where I am. This is my sanctuary. They will not dare harm me in my church.' That is where I left him, I hurried to you wearing the clothes when I entered the Sisterhood. Come! I know he will listen to you."

Tony hailed a cab. "We'll be at the church in fifteen minutes."

In the cab, Sister Clothilde took off her hat which she found uncomfortably unfamiliar, and leaned back. Grey streaks in her hair seemed to give her a careworn appearance. A demure face was marred by black rings under her eyes. She was sleepless and distressed, about the Monsignor. Her dress with a high collar waafted a whiff of mothballs which became strong in the cab. It embarrassed her, she fluffed her light coat to dispel the mothball vapors.

"Don't you think this an emergency. Mr. Di Napoli?"

"I'd say so. Lean back and relax."

"I forgot to change my convent shoes."

"It was a hike from the convent."

"I ran most of the way. I am afraid something dreadful will happen. I did not tell the sisters. I told them I was going to St. Jude's for text book samples."

"You did well."

The cab pulled up at the curb of St. Anne's. Tony headed for the baptistery near the tower to the right of the church. They stood before the bronze doors of the baptistery.

"John! This is Tony Di Napoli. I am here to help, open the door."

They heard the clang of tripped over brass candelabras.

"John, do you hear me."

"Tony! Two men followed me from Reno. They are going to kill me!"

"What happened at the casinos?"

"I played blackjack, I lost, my IOUs are worthless."

"How much did you lose?"

"I think 15, 16 thousand."

"Come out, we'll try to square it."

"I know you can, you have friends."

"Come out, John."

"Not before those killers leave! This is my sanctuary I can't leave!

"Sister Clothilde is with me."

"Bless her, bless her!"

"Ill take a look Father," Clothilde volunteered.

She went to the front of the church saw no one, and reported back to Tony.

"John, the street is empty." Tony banged on the bronze doors.

"Wait, I'll go up the baptistery tower to look for myself."

The baptistery was silent, then a clatter of heels as someone was vaulting the steps of the tower.

"You lied to me Tony! I can see them clearly in the shadow of the playground! They sent you! You say you are not a gangster, but you are! And you have Sister Clothilde cowering to help you to betray me."

"John, I'll go see for myself."

Tony walked in the direction of the playground and the two men shadowing the priest met him head on." One of them said: "Hello, Tony."

Tony recognized the men as enforcers for the bosses, "Hello, Maxie."

"Say hello to Freddy."

Tony waved a greeting. "Tell me Maxie, why the priest is in such a fix?"

"We got orders to waste him."

"A priest?"

"Freddy says he is going to do the Rosary when he hits him."

"What does he owe?"

"So far, with IOUs and shylocks seventy-five grand."

"He said 15,16 thou."

"Don't listen to him, he must be swell preacher, a good convincer, let's face it, Tony, he is a degenerate gambler. He talked to the dealers like he was the treasurer of the Vatican."

"Can you lay off for a while. When he comes to his senses, he'll make good."

"Tony, Tony, don't be an altar boy. This guy owes the shylocks on Essex Street about thirteen thou besides. That's almost a hundred grand. How can he make good? He thinks because he has a collar he ain't responsible?"

"Suppose you make a call to Reno, tell them you spoke to me, that I guarantee what he owes. Give me a couple of weeks."

"Are you serious?"

"My word."

"You are a man of respect. Even on the coast, they say you are the Prince of Policy. What a monicker! You're famous. Freddy call Reno, tell them what Tony says."

Freddy walked to the nearest phone booth and made the call, minutes later he was back. "Okay, two weeks."

When Tony got back to the baptistery he told Monsignor Keenan that the hit was off, he could come out, it was safe he would have time to repay.

The door opened, the smell of urine drifted into the church. Tony did not recognize him. He saw a grinning idiot, a broken, mumbling man, a wreck in the grip of a calamitous breakdown.

"What do we do now?" Clothilde leaned against the wall feeling faint.

"I'll wash him, you get his clothes."

"I am not allowed in his quarters."

"How about the robes for the Mass."

"In a closet, off the altar. I'll get them." A faucet nearby filled the font, Tony began to clean the gibbering priest.

When Monsignor Keenan was clean and in his vestments, he looked even more pitiable. "Here is our plan, Sister Clothilde, call the Archdiocese, tell them Monsignor John Keenan had a nervous breakdown, would they recommend a suitable psychiatric facility known to the Archdiocese. The Monsignor must be committed."

Sister Clothilde returned a half hour later. She spoke to an auxiliary bishop who suggested Stamford Hall in Connecticut. Sister Clothilde hailed a cab off the street, Tony hustled the priest into it, and Tony made arrangements with the driver about the long distance fare. Monsignor Keenan sat between them as the cab sped away from the curb. He lolled in his seat, the two had to push him off. Caught up in the excitement, Tony forgot the time, it was four thirty, he could never make it, get back to his flat, slip into the tux, and pick up Rachel at six. No way. He could not leave Sister Clothilde alone with the Monsignor, only he can deliver him to the institution. They arrived at 6 in the evening. The priest was immediately sedated and wheeled into a bright room. Sister Clothilde took care of all the admitting paper work. It was nine o'clock when the same cab, waiting, sped them back to the city.

In the cab, Sister Clothilde supported the borrowed vestments on her lap. Tony lit up a Russian cigarette.

"That cigarette is so fragrant."

"I buy them in a tobacco shop on Second Avenue, full of Byzantine crosses, and oleographs of old Russia."

"I read in a Russian novel that ballerinas smoked much before our time."

Tony thought of the dancers at the Kretchma who smoked pipefuls of oily Macedonian tobacco that soiled his carpet. "I think so."

"I am very partial to the fragrance of tobacco."

Tony had a hunch. "Do you smoke?"

"Rarely, only when Monsignor Keenan leaves a cigarette about, or a butt."

"A butt?"

"At times, he clinches a cigarette only half smoked. It is not a habit with me, you see it is tacitly frowned upon, if not actually forbidden." Tony took out his case and offered her the tapered and oval cigarette. He lit it for her. She took a long drag, inhaling. Tony figured she was a secret smoker. Either the priest forgave her smoking, or allowed his pack to be lifted.

Tony opened a window, the evening was starry.

The cigarette relaxed her. "Will he get better?"

"I think so, it will be just a bad episode in his life."

"He is bound for a splendid career. He is an authority on canon law. I typed many of his papers."

"You were close to him in his research."

"He is brilliant. He said you are a genius at math. I used to watch the two of you playing handball from my window and wished I could referee."

"I tell you Sister Clothilde, he cheated," he said laughing.

"I thought you shaved a few winners."

"Who were you rooting for?"

"I couldn't make up my mind, one day is was you, another him."

They were joshing, easing off the tension of the last seven hours. Finally she asked, "Can you save him?"

"I think so. I'll have to be gone for a while."

"To bargain for his life?"

"Something like that. In the meantime, he is safe where he is getting the treatment he needs. Don't allow him to discharge himself. You know what is waiting for him."

"Is addiction like love, an attachment to something or someone?"

Tony looked quizzically at Sister Clothilde in the dimness of the cab. "Funny you should ask that question You are married to Christ. Is that love or an addiction?"

"It's a conundrum, Tony. Pass me another cigarette. When you are gone, I and the sisterhood will be praying for you both. How will I get in touch with you?"

"You can't."

She lit the cigarette. "Please take care, I value your life as much as I do his."

"You do?"

"You two are the best handball players around," she quipped.

CHAPTER 20

Tony was at the airport when he called Rachel to tell her he would be gone for a week or so, and to apologize for the no show the night before. Never mind! She was taking a cab then, and there, to meet him at the airport no ifs or buts.

"Where are you?" She insisted in tears. "What's your flight number? I have my dresser on the other phone ready to make a call for the same ticket."

"You can't come Rachel. It is dirty business."

"Dirty or clean I'll be there! Tony, Tony. I'm miserable without you. I missed you so much last night. I am desperately in love. I have told Morris. He says he will shoot himself. Do I care, I don't know. I love you! I love you."

His flight was called, he let the receiver down gently. Tony had disappeared! Don Capodiferro and Patsy Paglieri questioned everywhere for his whereabouts the airlines, no Tony Di Napoli! The Bosses sent an emissary to see Rachel, and she knew nothing, they checked with St. Anne's, Monsignor Keenan was under medical care, that nun was in clausura and that meant silence and isolation. Patsy said, "Tony's trouble was women, always cunt in the mix of things, first fucking the widow in the coach, then that cockteaser from Montana Clarise when Tony came close to losing his balls, along comes black Edna causing Dutch Schultz conniptions and the cost of a steamship ticket to Paris, without stopping for breath, the tabloid sheet scandal with the Jew actress, forcing proud rabbis to ask for an audience with Don Capodiferro! And what's what now with the jazzy nun? Jesus Christ! A woman is a woman even if she dresses different. He hears that Sister Clothilde smokes and secretly plays handball. Tony is on the lam. Why didn't he speak to Don Capodiferro or his friend Patsy? Smartass first he puts the priest in that sanitarium out of reach of a enforcers by promising to pay the markers. He and the nun get the priest out of reach of a hit by putting him in a hospital, then Tony disappears when he made a promise to the boys that the priest would make good in two weeks, then he is gone. Where? Two weeks are almost up. Who is going to make the priests markers? God? But why did he go out of his way like a schmuck!? Patsy did not need to spell it out, it was the talk of the East Side!

On the eleventh day of Tony's departure the nun phones Patsy to tell him that Tony got in touch with her, he is back in town. He would meet Patsy at his place that afternoon. And she hung up.

Tony was early. He had a light tan.

"So you go sunning yourself when you not whoring around."

"My first vacation in five years. Patsy, what is your beef?"

"My beef? Seventy-thou in casino markers, and fifteen big ones, shylock that priest owes, and you co-signer!"

"I though it was all settled before I left, I spoke to the Archdiocese, they promised to make good for the Monsignor."

"Tony, first time in life you lie to me!"

"Not lying, Patsy. The Archdiocese is covering for him secretly. They don't want a scandal, it's got to be cash, no record."

"So where is the dough?"

"Here, in my pocket, it was delivered to me as I got off the plane." Tony withdrew a bulky envelope from his coat pocket

Patsy wiped his brow. "You give me stroke worrying about you. The bosses all set to call a sit down on you, you know what that means!"

"Here's the money, no sit down, right?

"Right as the rain from a merciful heaven." He embraced Tony. "Antonio, you mean a lot to me and the Don. Behave for God's sake, get married, stop whoring around. The Don took a fit when his wife saw you and the nun on Delancey Street, and the nun wear no habit! He goes to St. Anne's every Sunday. Jesus! Behave, Tony, keep your pecker in your pants, don't start lifting skirts of nuns, whatever they wear! Whew! I am going to payoff the shylocks and wire the money to Reno. What are you going to do?"

"I am going whoring, Patsy isn't that what you think?"

"No whoremaster, Tony, sorry I said it, the ladies come on to you strong, a prick has no conscience. I was young once. Come on, give me a kiss thank God, you are home safe."—

Tony took a cab to theatre which was empty. No one anywhere, he saw a sign that explained the closing on the holiday of Yom Kippur the Day of Atonement. He walked rapidly to the synagogue, the worshipers were exiting, he waited, then he saw Rachel and Morris on the top steps She turned to reenter the synagogue, not to meet him, hesitated, then slowly descended. Morris went by him without a glance. At the foot of the last steps they met, he tried to kiss her, she stepped back and averted her face.

"What's wrong, Rachel, I can explain everything."

"What's wrong, Tony? Everything! Everything! I don't say it's your fault, it's mine, too."

"Rachel! I love you!"

She fell on his neck weeping. "And I love you, Tony."

"Then what's to stop us—?"

She wiped her eyes with her satin gloves. "Before you left I told Morris I loved you, I was leaving him for you. He said nothing, you know what he is like. That night he took an overdose. People say I almost killed him, I am the whore of Babylon. The rabbi hemmed and hawed when I asked if I could come to the services. You know I am not a whore, Tony."

Tony kissed her gloved hands.

"It is Morris, he is a talented man like you, that's my weakness, talent."

"Rachel, man and woman who love each other, that's the divine equation."

"He finally got that offer to do a screenplay about Moses, we are leaving tonight."

"Pity is not love, Rachel, it won't last, you will end hating for holding you back from me and your life."

"His mother and father came to the hospital. Both placed curses on my head if I ever left him."

"Superstitions!"

"They broke my heart, Tony. It wasn't the curses."

"I will follow you!"

"No, no Tony, who knows a day may come when I shall weaken and ask you to fall into my arms."

A cab with Morris pulled up abruptly, the door was open. Rachel slipped into a seat, and Morris ordered the cab on.

Tony watched the cab disappear in the distance, then drop away from sight. He felt like punching a wall, pick up a manhole cover and roll it down the street smashing against parked autos, he kicked at a lamp post, smacked a telephone pole.

So it was no surprise to see Tony chest bared again slapping a loose spaldeen against the backboard of the playground. He did not see Sister Clothilde, in her habit, in position to his right, he just missed her with a swing at the ball. She returned the ball holding a ping pong paddle in her volleying hand. They volleyed silently.

Sister Clothilde spoke in rhythm to her swings: "Many an afternoon I watched you and John play. I rooted for him one day, another day for you. I am not a constant fan, I am afraid." She caught the rebounding ball on the fly, held it. "Is it a greater sin to love you, or a priest?" she said disarmingly.

Tony accepted what she said as a quip about her indecision about whom to vote for in a match. "John, and I will have a playoff and you can choose then."

"Suppose you are in love with both men?" She dropped the ping pong paddle, took his free hand and cupped it in hers.

Tony saw a sacrilegious infatuation in her eyes. He avoided eye contact, freed his hand, began to volley again. "I am driving out to see John, to tell him the good news. How is he?"

Sister Clothlde's hands reached up to her face, she turned her back to him." He is under mild sedation." Her voice was breathless, both arms crossed tightly against her breast to smother another impulsive indiscretion.

"Are you coming?"

"I-I am in charge of a Novena this evening."

"Who knows, he may be well enough so I can bring him back tonight."

Sister walked off slowly, "That would be nice."

Tony walked off for a short distance, when he stopped to wave so long, he saw Sister Clothilde in full face. She had gouged red cicatrices down her cheeks. Tony thought, that is why there are no mirrors in convents.

CHAPTER 21

Tony had garaged his Packard at Patsy's garage. He walked the short distance. Patsy was in his office.

"Where you been?"

"Playing handball."

"At a time like this?"

"Well, the crisis is over, isn't it."

"Yeah, sure, trying to touch base with you. The bosses got into heads to audit the policy and lottery plays for five years. Three men working while you were gone."

"And—?"

"Clean bill of health."

"Patsy, I need the keys to my car, I'm driving up to Connecticut to visit Monsignor Keenan."

"Hanging on the hook in the hallway. Tony, maybe you drop me off at Calvary, on way, got to register a grave."

"I can use the company."

"First, I got make phone call."

"I'll warm up the car."

Both men were lost in thought. When they got to the Kosciowski Bridge they began talking of old times. When Calvary Cemetery hove in sight, Patsy asked Tony to turn into a lane leading to Fifth

Calvary. The sun was setting in violent colors over offending bill-
boards, and industrial signs.

"I thought you are going to the office?"

"Too late, if you don't mind keep driving to Fifth Calvary. I have
to locate the grave."

"No problem, Patsy."

The Packard sped through the narrow lanes to Fifth Calvary.
Scarred like a battleground, the turf was plowed by earth movers, not
one headstone standing.

"What happened, Patsy?"

"Making room. Every hundred years cemetery is plowed for
another generation."

"Where is the grave you are looking for?"

Patsy was wiping his eyes, he was crying. He sobbed. "Here."

"What is it Patsy, someone you knew way back"

Patsy put his handkerchief back in his pocket. "It's getting dark"
said Tony.

"Tony, do you have a God?"

I've been looking for him"

"Number one?"

"Something like that, Patsy."

"Do you pray?"

"I think of Tessie."

"Tony! Tony!" Patsy banged his hat against his knee. "I spoke for
you. I was out voted! Why, why bail out that priest fly to Havana,
beat the bank for seventy-five thou? Why The priest don't deserve it!
A suicidal gambler! *Degenerato!* After while, didn't think you would
be recognized in Havana. You know you are not to play in any casino
anywhere in the world if you are a card counter, you are the best that
is, or was. You beat them. Sure, you could have broke the bank.
Bosses get suspicious. Braunstein plants hot shot accountants at your
office. Not only you beat Havana seventy-five grand, you fix the lottery and policy plays years. No, not for self you make the poor to

win, every church, every synagogue win on East Side, cut no dice with the bosses, even if ahead. Tony, guys at the sit down I never met, Cleveland, Chicago, Detroit, Los Angeles. Don't know you, Tony. You skim three million dollars spread over the East Side like honey. Tony, I love you what you did! But who me? Nobody compared to these big guns. They call a sit down, they put you down, but Don Capodiferro, make up his mind tomorrow. His wife don't like you. But you stupid, they find paper all over flat, million plays of lottery, you fix up the erase then you put back to make things correct that's how they catch you. You erase, they know nothing, you want to be big *professore* so you get caught."

Tony saw clearly now what happened, they came upon his calculations from a million plays in the lottery that expressed the aspirations and dream life in the lives of East Siders, to create a statistical profile of the East Side and its people and to predict probabilities. When he allowed certain slips to win he made erasure, then for purposes of statistics, he restored the true play, this gave him away. It is not true he retained everything in his mind, he transcribed for the purposes to create a very human awake and dreaming profile of his co-neighbors, of the East Side. Or a common soul?

"Why did you bring me here Patsy, are you going to blast me, carry out the verdict of the court? You? Sure, I am guilty, Patsy. Did they look at my bank account. I got zilch, never a cent for me."

"That's what I told them. I pleaded, on my knees! Take *Povero* Ignazio to your flat, say what do you see Ignazio? I see, Patsy, a big cardboard *tombola*, lottery card in corner, in closets and desk all plays of lottery seven years, numbers reach heaven, ask Ignazio what all mean, he say I don't know, they hit pistola, break jaw, Ignazio say Tony make study of players of East Side to see carattere, then pistola Ignazio again, he say you make lot of people win when they lose, maybe three million dollars. But you no got money in bank."

"What did they do with graphs and statistics?"

"They burn them say government prove income tax, all paper. But, Tony, why the *smorfia*, put down all the *numeri* and the dreams, wishes, curses of the people, why?"

Tony was shaken by the news of the shredding, more so by evidence of his uncovered complicity to help the needy and distressed of the East Side. For seven years, the formulation was his secret, the true reason why he remained on the job. In beginning, he asked himself what if he graphed or created a probabilistic equation for the lives of the East Side through the lottery play, the numbers based on millions and millions of dreams, hunches, moods, hopes, desperation until the lottery became a gigantic dream book. Would it reveal a model character of the people, a probability exercise, or the outcome be a study of the subconscious as revealed in dreams, hunches, secret desires, a psychoanalytic study surpassing any such attempt in the past. The East Side under analysis! He came to no conclusion, a study never to be. All was destroyed, chance or necessity? No backup files. He teetered against an upended headstone.

As for his fate, the Don, and the kangaroo courts must be reasonable, logical—although he biased the plays to succor the poor and ill of the East Side, to support the needy churches, temples, and charities, yes it is true he never skimmed for personal gain or profit. They will, after cooling down, forgive and forget. Besides, the winnings were the greatest haul ever in the history of the lottery and policy.

"You picked a hell of a place to tell me all this. Let's turn back I'll plead my own case."

"Tony, it's too late. A guy out there with a high-powered rifle. When I raise my hand—waits for me to raise my hand…"

Tony smiled grimly. "Of all people, you Patsy."

"Tony, as I am talking to you, a guy in my house pointing a gun at wife, and two daughters."

"Braunstein, he no wait for decision of the Don. He put you down! He send man to my house to give me phone number to set you up, his gun pointing at my wife, daughters, now I speak!"

"Where is he."

"Out there."

Tony saw only displaced earth, uprooted coffins on end, the night lights of earthmovers blinking, splintered planks spanned pits of seepage, a grey mist hovered over the bared graves like a blanket to cover a nakedness.

"Patsy remember that winter I was driving for you, we stopped at Loughrans for a hair on the dog. I felt sorry for the young widow bride, you saw see-sawing springs, you figured right. When it was time to go, you flicked me with your whip, and said 'Bad boy!' Have I grown up to be a bad man, Patsy?"

"*Amor di Dio*, no! Tony, you good, good man!"

In the late October sky reddened by the spoked rays of a setting sun, Tony saw a cluster of pink clouds, ten in all. Soon the sky will be velvet black, the infinite stars glittering in numbers, as number, did they exist, these numbers independently of us, or products of our minds? With the crack of that rifle yards away, will he know the answer? What would the afterlife be in either case? If there is Great Mathematician as the source of all phenomena, he thanked him for freely casting ten clouds across the sky. Or did he use a dice box? He fingered Teresa's medallion on his breast, and gripped it.

"Patsy, my favorite number is ten, did you know that?"

"No, Antonio mio bello."

"There are ten clouds in the sky. I am going to count the clouds up to ten, then you raise your hand as the signal."

"Where?" Patsy couldn't see, he peered. "I do see, Antonio, I do. Chi sa? Una grazia."

"Patsy. I am beginning to count the clouds—one, two, three, four, five, six, seven, eight, nine, ten—Patsy!"

Patsy raised his hand jerkily.

A whine, and a sharp report.

Tony was standing.

Patsy was sprawled on the earth in a dead faint. Tony was allowing one shot. He fell to his knees besides Patsy, drew a stone marker close as a shield for both. Patsy coming to stared at Tony as if was a ghost. Tony heard a crunch of footstep near his head. Rifleman at closer range! Tony rose like a rocket and barged into the broad chest of Don Capodiferro.

"Easy, Antonio, no Braunstein shooter, he no more." That whining bullet was meat for Gladstone's shooter beaten to the punch. He leaned against the chest of Capodiferro.

"No fraid no more, Antonio. I say you come back to family, you pay back casino. Yes, but swear you no fucky—fucky with nun like my wife say.

"No, on my word of honor."

"*Basta la parola.*"

Patsy was on his feet, embarrassed, he pissed himself.

"Antonio, take Patsy home, he need diaper."

"You saved my life."

"You are a *genio*. You go to flat, no go out. Patsy phone all clear. Have sit down with Gus Braunstein tonight, *capisce*. You no move, Patsy phone."

"I am sorry I crossed you—"

Don Capodiferro stared at him, bemused, "Trust? Is only a word. No double cross. People East Side like you, I like you, *capisce*. Nobody understand *genio*. Now, let's get out of cemetery. Braunstein's shooter fall in empty grave. *Via tutti!*"

Tony got back to a flat in shambles. Disorder matched the order in which his research had been collected.

He hardly got the door open blocked by a mound of shredded paper that filled three quarters of his studio flat, a cenotaph of paper, the shredding machine alongside. Here, to the mound, the mobsters added every sheet of paper, his computations, the lottery, policy bets of the East Siders, working equations, a probability index, personal files, Teresa's letters to him, personal notes passed between him, and Rachel, Clarisse. Edna, too his jaunty correspondence with the Monsignor, photographs of Teresa, his father Dominick, his mother. His books too, were macerated into this quivering pulp filling his flat. Why did all take on this shape?

Two million entries of bets now pulp. His dream of actualization of the Dream Book vanished like a poet's vision. Was he a planted poet, no scientist? Sight of the room in chaos tried the question as moot. He attempted to put things in place, could not, overcome by an exhaustion that forced him to lie on his rent couch in nervous collapse interrupted by day and night terrors of dissolution and despair in a room that now reflected a universal chaos. Panic, anxiety made him sweat cold and smelly. And still no phone call from Patsy freeing him from what was now a cell. On the third day, he had presence of mind to phone St. Anne's, he was told the Monsignor was still at the clinic, Sister Clothilde was on leave to visit her parents in the Maritimes…

He could not stay another moment in that room so redolent of failure. The day was sunny. His walk led him to Patsy's place.

"Tony, you look like you got killed and dug up. Relax, we have game of scoppa and drink the new wine of May. New wine, new life, Don Capodiferro say you go back to school, that's where a *genio* belongs."

"Patsy, I am lost."

"Not yet, we play *scoppa*, then you lose. Taste my wine.

Patsy poured from battered bottle used time and time again every year for new vintage. He filled two rough tumblers.

"*Bevi!*" said Patsy.

The wine freshly fermented bubbled on his tongue, he downed the glass. "Refreshing, Patsy. A good year."

"That's what I say Tony, drink up, and now sco*pp*a."

Patsy drew a new deck of cards from his desk, unwrapped the surrounding foil, and began to deal. After the third hand, the joker appeared which Patsy had forgotten to remove from the pack before playing. No joker in *scoppa*. Patsy was about to take the joker out of place, out of play. Tony's hand seized his with such strength that Patsy's arthritic fingers caused him to yelp. Tony was looking at the joker like he saw a snake.

"Tony, what's wrong? You can't play the joker."

"I know," said Tony, eyes shining hard.

"The joker plays itself, whatever it is or wishes to be."

A burst of uproarious laughter broke from Tony's lips. "What a blind fool I am. Here in a deck of cards I found my joker, that impersonator, that caprice, that blind or chance, that fate in our lives, that secret lies in a deck of cards—the joker!"

"All I know," said Patsy "I made *scoppa*, you lose."

Tony picked up the joker card, slipped it in his breast pocket. He smiled "Not yet, Tony, not yet." And he tapped his glass for more wine.

When Tony DiNapoli got back to his flat, the mound of shredded paper plays was increasingly friable. Tony slipped the joker card into the yellowing shreds, perhaps that cosmic joker, that jester, could make sense of the heap, as the activator of a timeless play, the protean player, the impersonator, the radical card in the deck, who mocks him, and his efforts, who escaped his trap of an equation. He stared at the combustible mound for hours waiting to catch fire, so that a phoenix, embodying all the lottery lives, and paper ashes of Casimir's portraits on the wind, would rise to a questionable heaven. Or set fire to it with a opium taper, and allow all to smolder into stupefaction? Was a sensuous equation a poppy dream after all? No. His East Siders were more meaningful than ever.

He escaped from the closeness of the room to the roof, the sun was dipping, across the surrounding tenement roofs clothes lines were flapping. Soon the women would be home from sweat shops and gather in the wash, Across the expanse of hundreds of clothes-lines, flapping wash stretched widely like sails of boats grounded in an inland sea.

Tony felt his throat tighten, his chest began to heave, he felt a stab under his heart, he burst into tears, a dam had given way, he was weeping. His face, his shirt, were wet with tears. Why was he weep-ing, not crying, as the faces of the sitters at the bathhouse appeared before his reddened eyes as in a gray mist over the East River? No! If he was crying out of pity, they did not need his pity, nor did they ever ask for his equation. He stepped over an airway on to an abut-ting tenement roof He wiped his eyes with a corner of a shift dan-gling on a clothesline. He strode or stepped on one roof to another. Roof tar was hard under his shoes, a remembered sign of autumn to a tenant From a squat chimney, a lazy curl of smoke scented of spicy cinnamon, and the tang of peeled fresh apples. Apple pie. At a stove pipe chimney, he heard a scratchy song from a Victrola, at another, a gaping chimney, the squalling of a baby. 57, fruit, 39, a song, 43, a baby. Dark now, too dangerous to retrace his steps over the roofs. A roof door was open, he entered, and descended the dim stairways. On the third landing, he bumped into Funzi, one of his lottery run-ners.

"Mr. Di Napoli! You!"

Funzi was unmistakeable, not Tony. In his sixties, he wore at all times a flashily hued jacket, he fluttered up and down the gas lit landings like a bespectacled moth. He took off his thick lens glasses and peered at Tony.

"It's me, Funzi."

"Geez!"

"Funzi, I want to play the numbers 57, 39, and 43 in terno for a dollar."

Funzi pencils hovered over a slip of paper, not sure if Tony was serious.

"Write it down, Funzi,"

"Whatever you say, Mr. Di Napoli."

Tony walked past the astonished Funzie, down three flights to the entrance door, and out to a littered sidewalk. He stood by under a flickering lamp post as push cart after push cart tracked. home. He stopped a push cart half-loaded with fruit and bought an apple, a Macintosh, sugary and frosted, and gnawed it until the parade of push carts turned the corner. He clinched the lottery slip in his fingers: 57,39,43. First thing tomorrow, he will apply at City College for that promised fellowship in the Department of Higher Mathematics.

FINIS

0-595-27105-7